Rodeo Rescue

Mary Blakeslee

For Joan Marshall
with love

Published by: Overlea House
20 Torbay Road
Markham, Ontario
Canada L3R 1G6

Cover art: Gary McLaughlin

R.L.: 4-6

Canadian Cataloguing in Publication Data

Blakeslee, Mary
Rodeo rescue

ISBN 0-7172-2397-3 (bound) ISBN 0-7172-2475-9 (pbk.)

I. Title.

PS8553.L34R62 1988 jC813'.54 C88-094607-5
PZ7.B58Ro 1988

123456789 WC 7654321098

Printed and Bound in Canada.

CHAPTER 1

Tina leaned forward so she could see past the crowd lining the parade route. The first marching band and the car carrying the Stampede officials had gone by. Now the Stampede Queen and her two princesses were approaching on horseback. As they came to where she stood with her twin brother, Ted, and her cousins, Hal and Trish Jacobs, the kids all let out a wild "Yahoo! Way to go, Amy!"

One of the princesses was Tina's sister, Amy. She waved and threw them a kiss. Tina waved excitedly back. Then as her eye travelled to the float following the royal group, she saw a woman standing across the street beside a grocery cart filled with pop cans. The woman, dressed all in black, was glaring at the girl who was Stampede Queen. The look on her face was frightening: anger tinged with madness. Tina felt a cold shiver go down her back as she watched the woman's eyes follow the entourage down the street. When the royal trio was out of sight the woman pushed her way ungraciously back through the crowd and disappeared.

"Did you see that strange person with the grocery cart?" she asked Trish in a hushed voice.

"What person?" Trish answered vaguely before rushing on. "Oh, didn't Amy look beautiful? And Helen! She's like a tiny angel. No wonder they picked her out of all those girls to be queen this year." She sighed. "Someday *I'm* going to be Stampede Queen, just you wait and see."

"Yeah, and I'm going to be a champion bronco rider," her brother Hal put in as he reloaded his camera. "Come on, Trish, you have to be able to ride a horse to be Stampede Queen and you're scared to get within ten metres of one."

"Hey, look, here comes a bunch of those miniature horses. Maybe you could ride one of those in the parade," Ted suggested.

Trish gave him a scathing look and turned haughtily away. Tina joined in the boys' laughter but her mind was still on the woman with the hostile stare.

The kids stayed until the last float went by nearly three hours later then headed for the Palliser Hotel, where they'd arranged to meet the twins' mother and father.

George and Grace Harper had invited the twins' cousins from Toronto to come to Calgary for the annual Exhibition and Stampede. Trish and Hal had seen the parade and the chuckwagon races and the infield events on television, but they had never seen the *Greatest Outdoor Show on Earth* live. So when the invitation had come for them to stay with the Harpers for the whole ten days, they jumped at the chance. Hal was the same age as the twins, and a great guy when his mind wasn't on food. Trish, a year younger at eleven going on twenty, would have fitted in better at a fashion show, but still she was a pretty good sport.

"Well, how did you like the parade?" Mr. Harper asked as they sat around a table in the hotel's coffee shop.

"It was great!" Hal enthused. "A lot better than seeing it on the tube."

"What did you like best?" Mrs. Harper

smiled across at their excited faces.

"The Indians!" Ted cried.

Hal disagreed. "The antique cars!"

"I liked the floats with the beautiful girls." Trish gazed off into the distance with the dreamy look that told everyone she was seeing herself dressed in a gorgeous outfit, riding in the parade.

"I loved everything," Tina said smiling. Then she remembered the frightening woman. "Mom, there was this weird woman at the parade with a whole grocery cart full of pop cans. What on earth would she be doing with them?"

"Collecting them to sell, probably," her mother answered. "There are a lot of those women—and men, too—who hang around where crowds have gathered to pick up the discarded cans. It's really quite sad."

"Calgary's answer to the New York bag lady," Mr. Harper muttered. "The woman probably has a fortune stashed away under a dirty mattress somewhere."

"Now, George, that's hardly fair. The poor thing may have to rely on what she can collect to buy food. The recession has caused a lot of people to do strange things to survive."

"Hmpf!" snorted her husband. Dismissing the subject he picked up the menu and glanced down at it. "Okay, who's for the special?" he asked.

Everyone began to check the offerings, and Tina's strange woman was soon forgotten. For the time being, at any rate.

When they had finished eating, Hal leaned back in his chair and yawned. "Gee, I don't know whether it's the food or the excitement, but I'm pooped."

"It probably has something to do with the fact that you got in at one-thirty this morning and didn't get a wink of sleep the whole night," his aunt grinned. "I think the best thing for you kids to do is come home with me and have a nice long nap. Your uncle has to get back to work, but tomorrow we're all going to Stampede Park early."

"Sounds good to me," Trish nodded. "Will we get to see Amy?"

"Well, it's hard to say. Amy and the other two girls are staying with their chaperone at a hotel the Stampede Board reserved for them. They're going to be kept very busy all during the Stampede, but I'm hoping Amy will have some time off to see you."

"That's super!" Trish gushed. "Maybe she can give me some pointers on getting picked to be a princess—or the queen."

Ted gave her a disgusted look and muttered, "Fat chance."

Sensing a flare-up between her brother and her cousin, Tina got up from her chair and said, "Okay, let's go. I'm really bushed."

Mrs. Harper nodded and they left the twins' father to pay the bill while they walked to the parking lot elevator.

* * *

"How come Amy has to stay at a hotel, Aunt Grace?" Trish wanted to know.

The cousins were just sitting down to a late evening supper.

"It's easier if the girls are all together," her aunt answered, passing a plate of cold chicken down the table. "They have to be up by six in the morning and are often on the go until midnight, so it's just practical for them to be in the same place. Besides, Helen doesn't live in town, you know. She comes from a ranch out near Cochrane."

No one spoke for the next ten minutes as the kids proceeded to demolish every scrap of food on the table. Finally, Trish wiped her mouth and sighed.

"I think it's so romantic that Helen's boyfriend is a cowboy."

"He's not really a cowboy, Trish," her aunt pointed out. "He owns his own ranch out near where Helen lives. But he does take part in the local rodeos when he can get the time. He used to be a rodeo performer full-time before his father died and he took over the ranch."

"Is he going to be competing in the Stampede?" Tina asked.

"I think Amy said he was entering the saddle bronc riding event."

"Wow!" Hal and Ted cried in unison.

"Do you think we might get to meet him?" Hal asked.

"We'll see. Now if you kids are all through, why don't you watch the chuck-wagon races on TV. They should be starting about now."

The kids trouped into the den and turned on the television just as the first heat was being announced. It was exciting, but they knew it was nothing compared to actually being right there at the track. Well, that would happen tomorrow.

They watched a rerun of an old western when the chucks were over, then turned back to the local station to see the highlights of the afternoon's infield events.

"What's Helen's boyfriend's name,

Mom?'' Tina called out when the saddle bronc event came on.

''Nick Gilbert,'' came the answer from the kitchen.

They all watched closely, hoping to see Nick, but his name wasn't called.

''They only ride two days out of the first eight.'' Mrs. Harper appeared at the door wiping her hands. ''He might not be riding till tomorrow or even the next day. I understand they draw for days.''

As the recap of the day's events finished, Trish stood up and yawned.

''I'm for bed. I was so wound up I didn't really sleep much this afternoon and I want to be wide awake tomorrow. It should be really exciting.''

Little did she know how exciting it really would be!

CHAPTER 2

"Come on, Tina," Ted called. "Mom's waiting for us. It's almost ten-thirty—the day's practically over—and you're sitting around staring at the boob tube!"

"Trish is still in the bathroom," Tina answered without taking her eyes off the screen. "We were watching this channel that covers the stuff going on downtown while we waited for you and Hal to finish your *third* stack of pancakes." She rolled her eyes and puffed her cheeks out. "Then Helen and Amy and the other princess came on. See, there they are now." She pointed to the screen where a man in a cowboy hat was standing on a platform in the middle of the Stephan Avenue Mall talking to the three girls.

"So?" Ted raised an eyebrow. "Did that make Trish have to go to the john?"

Tina laughed and shook her head. "No, dope. But when she saw the way Helen was wearing her hair she rushed off to copy it. Don't panic. She'll be out in a min—" She broke off and stared hard at the TV set. "Ted, look! It's that woman again. The one with the pop cans. See her behind the platform?"

Ted came over and peered at the set. "You mean that old bag in the long black dress?"

"Yeah. She's the same one I saw watching Helen at the parade yesterday."

"Boy, she looks scary. I'd hate to meet her in a dark alley!"

"That's exactly the way she looked yesterday—angry and frightening. Just look at the way she's staring at Helen."

At that moment the camera turned away from the platform and panned the crowd in the Olympic Plaza, better known as Rope Square during Stampede time. When it moved back to the announcer on the platform, the girls were gone. So was the woman in black.

"I don't like it, Ted. She looks like she could be dangerous."

"Who looks dangerous?" Trish came into the den adjusting her Stetson on her newly braided hair. Without waiting for an answer she twirled around in front of them. "Well, what do you think?"

"About what?" Ted wanted to know.

"My new hairdo. It's exactly like Helen's."

"Too bad the rest of you is so far off the mark." Ted laughed and ducked as Trish aimed the pointed toe of her new cowboy boot at his leg.

"Come on, you two, play nice." Tina switched off the television and walked over to the door. "Where's Hal?" she asked peering down the hall toward the kitchen. "He isn't still eating, is he?"

"Nah, he's already in the car. That is, unless he's taking more pictures of the garbage cans or the hinges on the gate. Honestly, ever since he took that photography course last year he thinks he's Ansel Adams."

Tina giggled and took Trish's arm. "Well, maybe when Trish is crowned Miss Canada Hal can be her official photographer." Fortunately, Trish missed the wink Tina gave her brother.

"Finding a parking place anywhere near the Park is just about impossible," Mrs. Harper said as they drove along Twenty-fifth Avenue toward the south entrance to Stampede Park. "So I'll just drop you here where the buses unload and take the car back downtown. I'll pick your father up at his office and we'll come back to meet you at noon in front of the Roundup Centre." She brought the car to a halt and the kids piled out. Through the open car window she handed Ted an envelope. "Here are your tickets. They get you into the Park as well as into the grandstand for the afternoon rodeo. See you at noon. Have fun!" She waved and drove off.

The kids rushed over to the turnstiles, showed their tickets and ran across the bridge into the Park. A girl in an elaborate fringed skirt handed them a brochure with a map and a list of the main events of the day.

"Gee, there's so much to see and do," Trish exclaimed as she scanned the program. "Where do we start?"

"How about that stand up ahead where they're selling candy floss?" Hal suggested.

Trish made a gagging noise and Tina cried, "Hal, you just finished eating!"

"Well, okay," Hal grumbled, "but nobody seems to realize I'm a growing boy."

"Yeah, growing sideways," Trish murmured.

"It says here the pig races start in about fifteen minutes," Ted read, ignoring the bantering going on around him. "Gee, you guys have got to see them. They're really great."

"Yuk," Trish commented. "Couldn't we go to the Big Four Building and look at the exhibits instead?"

"I'd like to see the horse barns," Tina put in.

They stood in the middle of the path looking at each other.

"Look," Ted said at last, "we've got all week. We can see the exhibits and the horse barns anytime; the pig races only happen a few times a day."

"Okay," Tina agreed. "The pig races it is. But we'd better hurry. They're way down at the other end of the Park."

After they had watched the hilarious little pigs race around the enclosure to the yells of an enthusiastic crowd, they wandered over to the midway and took in all the exciting sights and sounds and smells. It was five minutes to twelve before Ted looked at his watch and exclaimed, "We'd better get moving. The

Roundup Centre isn't far off, but in this crowd it could take ages to get there."

When the group got to the entrance to the huge building, Mr. and Mrs. Harper were already there waiting for them.

"We can eat here if you like," Mrs. Harper suggested, "then walk over to the grandstand. The infield events start at one-thirty, but we have reserved tickets so we don't have to hurry."

"Sounds great!" Hal slung his camera over his shoulder and rubbed his hands together. "All this running around has given me an appetite."

"I would've thought the three candy apples you ate right after finishing the two ice cream sticks would have tamed your appetite," Tina grinned, patting his stomach where the buttons on his shirt had popped open.

"That sort of thing doesn't stay with you," Hal answered. "A man needs good red meat to keep up his strength."

"Come on," his uncle laughed. "We'd better get in and find seats before Hal passes out on us."

Hal nodded solemnly in agreement and followed his hysterical friends through the door and past the multitude of booths to the food fair at the back of the building.

"Will we see Amy today?" Trish asked eagerly when they had collected their food and were sitting at one of the crowded tables.

"Absolutely," her uncle answered. "The girls ride in the opening ceremony before the rodeo starts."

"I mean see her to talk to her." Trish's disappointment was hard to miss.

Mr. Harper's eyes twinkled as he looked at his niece. "Actually, I was keeping it for a surprise, but Amy will be joining us for dinner tonight. The girls have two hours off before they have to start their evening activities."

"Hey, that's terrific!" Ted shouted. "Wait'll you see Amy up close, Hal. She's a lot different than when you were here before."

"Yeah," his sister agreed. "She's really gorgeous."

Hal looked down at his plate piled high with rich food, then down at his gaping shirt front.

"Gee, I guess I'm not as hungry as I thought," he said, pushing his plate away.

No one said a word. They all just bent their heads over their plates trying to cover their grins. After a couple of minutes, Hal reached out and pulled his plate back.

"On second thought, girls like guys with a bit of bulk to them."

That afternoon, Helen and Amy and the other princess rode at the front of the procession opening the afternoon rodeo events. The cousins yelled themselves hoarse. Even Mr. and Mrs. Harper got into the act, cheering and waving like a couple of kids. Then the announcer and the rodeo clown did a bit of silly bantering while the officials got ready for the first event, championship buffalo riding. Right after that came the wild cow milking contest. It wasn't until the break before the bareback bronc riding event that anyone stopped to look at the program.

The clown and the announcer were joking around again when Trish suddenly exclaimed, "Look, Nick Gilbert's name is here under the Saddle Bronc Riding Championships. See, on the next page." She pointed to Tina's program. "There he is—number two."

The kids all peered at their programs and Hal said, "That's supposed to be about the most professional event in the rodeo. You have to be really good to win."

"You have to be really good to win any of the events, Hal," his uncle said. "Riders come from all over the States and Canada to take part in the Calgary Stampede."

"But saddle bronc riding must be really tough," Hal insisted.

The competition *was* tough. It took some very skilled riding for Nick to come out ahead. His score was 79, two points ahead of the runner-up.

"Of course, that doesn't mean too much," Mr. Harper warned them. "Nick has to ride one more time during the week and his total score has to be in the top fourteen to allow him to advance to the semi-finals on Saturday. If he places in the top five there, he will have to compete with the top five in the Pro Rodeo series on Sunday. Finally the top four contestants advance to the finals and a chance to win $50 000."

By the time the infield events were over at four-thirty, none of the kids was able to talk above a whisper. They had yelled and screamed their way through the calf roping, the bull riding, the barrel racing and all the other rodeo events that made up the afternoon's program. When the last event finished, they staggered out of the stands and went over to the main doors to wait for Amy.

"I don't think I could eat a thing, Aunt Grace," Trish complained. "I'm just too excited.''

''Don't worry, Trish. I'll eat your share,'' Hal croaked. Then as Amy Harper came toward them and he got a close-up of the twins' sister, his eyes got huge and he involuntarily sucked in his stomach. ''Then again,'' he sighed, ''maybe I won't.''

CHAPTER 3

"The most awful thing happened!" Amy cried as the group gathered round her. "We were at the Golden Acres Nursing Home visiting the residents when Helen got called to the phone. It was somebody from the Stampede office telling her that Nick had been badly hurt during the bronc riding event and had been taken to the hospital. We were only a few blocks away so she just took off. She didn't tell anyone. I guess she was afraid her aunt would hold her up."

"Her aunt?" Trish asked.

"Yes, her father's sister. She lives with them; she has ever since Helen's mother died when Helen was only four or so. She came into town to be with Helen during her reign as Stampede Queen."

Ted and Tina looked at one another, then at their mother and father. Mr. Harper stopped walking and took Amy by the arm.

"Are you telling us that Nick was hurt in the bronc riding competition?"

"That's right. Helen didn't stick around to give me any details; as a matter of fact, I wouldn't even have known about it except that I saw her leaving by the side door, and she told me what had happened."

"But that's impossible," Tina cried. "We saw Nick riding in the competition. He didn't get hurt; he got the highest marks, for Pete's sake!"

"Are you sure?" Amy looked confused. "It must have been someone else."

"No, look here." Ted opened his program and pointed to the list of contestants under the Saddle Bronc Riding competition. "See, the second name from the top: Nick Gilbert, Cochrane, Alberta. I put down his score: 79."

"But I don't understand," Amy peered at the program. "If he wasn't hurt why would anyone tell Helen he was?"

"Probably some ding-a-ling with a warped sense of humour," Hal said, shaking his head.

"Yeah, that's probably what it was," Ted agreed. "There are enough loony-tunes around, that's for sure."

"What a cruel joke for anyone to play on the poor girl," Mrs. Harper said. "It's enough of a strain being Stampede Queen without having someone pull that kind of a stunt."

"I wish I knew for sure she was okay." Amy looked worried. "But I have no idea how to get in touch with her or anyone else for that matter. We were all given time off and each of us went our own way. I don't even know where our chaperone is right now."

"Well, I'm sure Helen will show up in lots of time for the opening of the grandstand events this evening," said her mother soothingly. "Meanwhile, there's nothing we can do, so we might just as well have a good dinner and get caught up on the exciting details of your past couple of days."

"I guess you're right, Mom," Amy agreed, still looking worried. She tried to smile. "I can't wait to demolish a thick steak; I've had to practically starve myself to get into these tight pants." She took her two cousins by the arm. "Okay, you guys, tell me everything that's happened to you since I saw you three years ago. You have ten minutes to make a full report.''

They chatted non-stop as they drove down Seventeenth Avenue and parked across from a trendy-looking restaurant. As they were walking over to it, Tina suddenly grabbed Ted by the arm and pointed down the street.

''Ted, look! Isn't that the same bag lady we saw on TV; the one who was watching Helen so closely?''

Ted looked to where the woman was coming toward them pushing her grocery cart. Stuffed in the cart was what looked like a big, lumpy tarpaulin. ''It sure looks like her. She must've really got lucky today. There must be a zillion pop cans under that tarp.''

''Oh, Ted, what difference does . . . never mind.'' She turned around to tell her parents about the woman. ''See,'' she said, turning back. ''There she is down by the— She's gone!'' she cried. ''But she was there just a minute ago.''

''Well, don't worry about it, dear,'' her mother advised. ''She's just a poor soul probably living in a back room somewhere. Now, come on. Let's get moving. Amy doesn't have that much time.''

* * *

"So what do you have to do besides ride at the opening of the rodeo and be in the parade?" Trish asked Amy as they were sitting back waiting for the waitress to bring dessert.

"Oh, there are all kinds of public appearances we have to make: pancake breakfasts at shopping malls; visiting hospitals and nursing homes and clubs. We have a really tight schedule."

"Gee," Trish sighed. "But it must be wonderful. How do you get picked to be a princess or the queen?"

"It's a long process," Amy answered. "For me the hardest part was the impromptu speech we had to make. After that it was kind of fun. You're interviewed by the judges so they can get an idea of your personality. And of course your riding ability counts for a lot. The judges choose ten finalists, who then have to go to two dinners where they're really checked out. Finally, during the Rodeo Royal the three top girls are picked."

"It sounds hard! And you don't see much of your folks during Stampede time, I guess."

"That's for sure. But at least I can see my family a couple of times. Poor Helen has only her aunt and Nick."

"Why? Doesn't her father come into town for Stampede?"

"No way. He was furious when Helen entered the contest and he's even more furious that she won. Apparently he keeps her on a really tight rein; she can't go to parties or on week-end skiing trips or anything. It's amazing that she and Nick managed to get together at all."

"He sounds like a ogre," Tina remarked wrinkling her nose. "What's his problem?"

"Well, according to Helen, he became really strange after her mother died. She doesn't remember her mother at all. She's never even seen a picture of her—her dad destroyed them all."

The waitress came with the dessert cart, and the conversation turned to who would have what. Hal was unable to make up his mind between the German chocolate cake and the lemon pie so he had both.

"Honestly, Hal," Trish said, "you're going to go home looking like one of those little pigs we saw racing today—only bigger."

Hal gave her a dirty look, glanced at Amy to see how she was taking it, and pushed the lemon pie away.

"Nonsense," Amy disagreed. "Hal, you look just fine to me. And you're still growing; you need extra energy."

Hal looked over at Amy adoringly and

pulled the pie back.

"My sentiments exactly!" he answered around a mouth full of meringue.

* * *

Amy had to be back at the hotel by six-thirty to change before the evening performance, so as soon as the meal was finished the group left the restaurant. After dropping Amy, they headed back to the Park.

There was still plenty of time to take in a couple of rides before the chuckwagon races began. While Mr. and Mrs. Harper settled for the ferris wheel, the kids opted for the roller coaster. Unfortunately it wasn't a good choice for Hal. The minute the ride stopped he rushed for the nearest trashcan and separated his queasy stomach from the cake and pie.

His aunt was very concerned. "Do you want us to take you home, Hal?" she asked.

"Naw, I'll be fine. Now I've got room for a corn dog."

The other three kids groaned and Mr. Harper suggested they'd better get to the grandstand; the chuckwagon races would be starting in about five minutes.

The Harpers had seen the chucks many

times but it was a first for their cousins. There were nine heats in the Rangeland Derby, each with four rigs taking part and each more exciting than the one before it. Watching the start where the wagons circled the barrels before taking off around the track was thrilling enough, but seeing the four teams racing down the stretch, the driver sitting on the chuckwagon steering the four horses and his four outriders flanking him, was breathtaking.

"They must get really tired," Trish remarked as the contenders in the ninth heat took their positions. "How often do they have to compete?"

"Every night, Trish," her uncle replied. "The four rigs with the best accumulated times after the first nine days get to participate in the sudden death final next Sunday. The purse is $50 000, so they're all pretty serious."

The starting gun went off and the four rigs began their race around the barrels. As they came onto the main track their outriders joined them. All, that is, except one poor cowboy who managed to fall off his horse just as his team took off down the track. The horse kept on going, the rider chased along behind and the crowd screamed with delight.

Finally, the rider managed to catch up with the runaway, mount and tear after his team.

"The outriders have to be with the wagon at the finish line," Uncle George explained, "or else they lose points."

In no time the rigs were coming around the turn and heading for the finish line. The whole grandstand rose as one. The air was electric as the two lead teams roared past, neck and neck, with the other two just a few metres behind. Thirty-two horses running at top speed in such a confined space—it was awesome.

The sportscaster announced the unofficial times of the last heat and the grandstand began to empty.

"We've got a few minutes before the grandstand performance begins," Mrs. Harper said. "Anyone want anything?"

Hal had been so busy taking pictures during the chucks that he hadn't mentioned food at all. As he rewound the film and removed it from the camera he muttered, "I guess I could use a little something."

"I'll just bet you could," Trish remarked.

"We'll wait here for you, kids," Mr. Harper said. "But don't be gone too long. The show starts in a few minutes and you don't want to miss seeing Amy and the other girls."

After loading up on hot dogs, chips and drinks, the cousins returned to the grandstand just as the announcer was asking the crowd to stand for "O Canada."

They rushed up the aisle to their seats and stood at attention while the band played the national anthem.

"And now, here to welcome you to the grandstand show are your two Stampede princesses, Amy Harper and Rhonda Lassiter."

Amy and Rhonda bounced onto the stage to wild applause from the huge audience. As everyone around them clapped and whistled, the Harpers and their cousins sat in stunned disbelief. Finally, Tina whispered, "Helen's not there. Something's happened to her. I just know it."

CHAPTER 4

"Come on, we'll catch Amy when she and Rhonda leave the stage. We've got to find out what's happened."

Mr. Harper stood up and beckoned for the others to follow him. The two princesses had each said a few words to the crowd and were leaving the stage as the *Young Canadians* got ready for the opening number.

Amy and Rhonda, their chaperone and Helen's Aunt Charlotte were coming around the back of the grandstand heading for their car when Hal, Trish and the Harpers caught up with them.

"Amy," Mrs. Harper called as her daughter turned to meet them, "what happened to

Helen?''

''Oh, Mom!'' Amy looked ready to cry. ''We don't know. She didn't show up at the hotel, and when we phoned the hospital to see if they knew where she went, they told us she'd never arrived. We waited as long as we could, and then we had to go on without her.''

Rhonda and the chaperone were standing a little apart trying to calm down Helen's aunt. Amy gestured toward them and went on. ''Helen's aunt is absolutely beside herself. She thinks it's all her fault that Helen is missing, and she has to phone Helen's dad and tell him. I sure don't envy her that little task.''

The group started to move down the park to the north exit.

''Have the police been informed?'' her father asked.

''Yes, Miss Gaynor—that's Helen's aunt—called them as soon as she realized Helen was missing. The Stampede board is worried sick, of course, but they naturally want the whole thing kept as quiet as possible so that people won't panic. The police have agreed to co-operate by keeping the press out of it, for now at least.''

''Where are you off to now, Amy?'' Her

mother's voice was anxious.

"We're going back to the hotel. The police want to talk to all of us about what happened at the nursing home—not that we have much to tell them."

"Well, I don't like it. I think you should come home with us. If there's some sort of crazy kidnapper out there, you could be his next victim."

"Oh, Mom, don't be so dramatic! I'll be okay. After all, our chaperone is with us all the time, and someone from the Stampede board is always around when we go out. I promise I won't go off on my own like Helen did."

Rhonda and the older women had arrived at the car that was to take them to their hotel. When the others joined them, Amy performed the introductions.

"I'm so very sorry, Miss Gaynor," Mrs. Harper said. The distraught woman looked at her gratefully.

"Thank you," she said. "It's so—I don't usually come apart like this, but when I think of what poor Helen—and having to tell her father—" She began to cry again.

"Mom." Amy drew her mother aside. "Could Miss Gaynor maybe stay at our house until this is all cleared up? It will just make her more crazy to have to be at the hotel with us."

"I don't see why not, if it's all right with her."

"That's so very kind of you," Helen's aunt replied when Mrs. Harper extended the invitation. "I'll have to go with the girls to talk to the police, but if I could come over later . . . ?"

"Of course. I can come and get you," Mr. Harper offered. "Amy, you give us a call when the police are finished with you. We'll all be so anxious to hear any news."

"Will do," Amy agreed. "And thanks for taking Miss Gaynor. I know she'll be a lot better off with you—especially after she's broken the news to Helen's dad. She'll need all the moral support she can get."

* * *

"I'm sorry you missed the grandstand show, kids, but perhaps you can catch it another evening," Mrs. Harper said as she turned the heat on under the hot chocolate. "After all, you've still got a week before you go back home."

Mr. Harper had gone to collect Miss Gaynor, and the kids were sitting around the table in the kitchen waiting for them to return. The evening had been unusually cold, a mere 15°C, and everyone was a little chilled.

"I'm just as glad we left when we did," Trish said. "It was getting darned uncomfortable in the grandstand. Besides, I don't think we would have enjoyed the show much knowing something must have happened to Helen."

Mrs. Harper came over to the table and started pouring the chocolate. "Never mind, honey, the police will find her. And as for the weather, it'll probably hit thirty tomorrow. You know what they say about Calgary—if you don't like the weather, just wait ten minutes or cross town and you'll probably get what you want."

"If it is nice tomorrow will be going to the Park again?" Hal asked.

"Actually, I thought we'd take a break from the Stampede and all go up to Pine Lake for the day. We can have a picnic, and if it's warm enough you can spend the day in the water."

"Sounds great!" Hal cried. "What did you have in mind for the picnic?"

Before the groans had died down the front door opened and Mr. Harper with a very distraught Miss Gaynor in tow came into the house.

"Any word yet?" Mrs. Harper rushed over to meet them.

"No, nothing," Miss Gaynor sighed. "The police are checking all the houses in the area —not that there are very many—and rounding up various people for questioning, but so far they don't have any leads." She sank down in a empty chair at the table and looked vaguely around. "I suppose I'll have to phone my brother. I was praying Helen would be found before he had to know about the kidnapping."

"So the police think it's definitely a kidnapping, do they?" Mrs. Harper asked.

"Oh, yes. There's no other rational explanation."

"If you want to call your brother, there's a phone in the den you can use," Mr. Harper offered. "It's quite private."

"Yes, thank you very much," she answered without moving. A shudder passed over her and she bit her lip.

The kids looked at one another, then at Mr. and Mrs. Harper. It was pretty obvious that Helen's aunt was terrified of telling her brother about the disappearance.

"Would you like me to call for you, Miss

Gaynor?'' Mr. Harper offered in a gentle voice. ''You're very upset and not really in any condition to make the call yourself. I'm sure your brother would understand that.''

''You're very kind.'' Miss Gaynor smiled wanly. ''But I'd better do it myself.'' She stood up and visibly pulled herself together. ''If you don't mind, I'll use that phone right over there.''

She walked over to the phone on the wall beside the back door and dialed. A moment later a voice loud enough to be heard across the room came over the receiver.

''Yes? Who is it?''

''It's me, Arthur. I'm afraid I have some bad news.''

''Charlotte, is that you? Speak up, woman, I can hardly hear you.''

Miss Gaynor cleared her throat and repeated, ''I have some bad news.'' She hesitated a moment, then plunged on. ''It's Helen. She's disappeared.''

''What did you say? Helen's disappeared? What are you talking about?''

''She didn't come back to the hotel this evening and she wasn't at the grandstand show. She and the girls were—''

Before she could finish her explanation, Mr. Gaynor's voice roared over the receiver,

"She's gone off with that young fool, Nick Gilbert. I warned you, Charlotte. They've just been waiting for a chance to go off together."

"No, Arthur, Nick's right here and he's as worried as we are about Helen. You don't . . ." she began to cry and the phone slipped from her hand.

Mr. Harper rushed over and picked it up.

"Hello, Mr. Gaynor? This is George Harper. My daughter is a good friend of Helen's. She's one of Helen's princesses. Your sister is staying with us until this whole thing is cleared up. Now, I've talked to the police myself. They think it's a kidnapping and that you'll likely be receiving a ransom note sometime in the next day or two. They've suggested that you stay where you are and wait for it rather than coming into Calgary. We'll be keeping you posted on any new developments."

"Your daughter's one of the princesses, eh? Well, I hope you've got more control over her than I do over my girl. I warned her that if she insisted on going ahead with this Stampede Queen nonsense, something would happen to her." Without any word of acknowledgment about the arrangements, Mr. Gaynor slammed down the phone.

"How very strange," Mrs. Harper murmured as her husband hung up the receiver and turned a baffled face to the stunned group behind him.

"He didn't ask anything about what had happened," Ted exclaimed. "It was like he was expecting it all along."

"He's a very strange man," Charlotte Gaynor said. "He was furious when Helen was asked to enter the Stampede Queen contest; insisted it was just an excuse for her to flaunt herself before men. Then he said the one thing that seemed to give Helen the courage to go ahead with the contest despite his objections: 'You're just like your mother was'."

"Weird!" Hal exclaimed. "What was Helen's mom like, anyway?"

"She was lovely, Hal. Dark with blue eyes like Helen. I didn't know her very well, of course, since I was working in a hospital down in Florida when she and Arthur were married. When she died Arthur called me and asked if I could come up and look after little Helen until he could make other arrangements. He never did make any other arrangement, and I've been there ever since."

"Is he pretty rich?" Ted asked. His mother frowned and he went on to explain. "I mean, if someone kidnapped Helen for the ransom, then they must think her father's got lots of money."

"He's comfortable but I certainly wouldn't say rich. If there is a ransom demand and it's at all high, I don't know where he'll find the money."

Tina and Ted exchanged looks. The whole thing was getting curiouser and curiouser.

CHAPTER 5

Just as Mrs. Harper predicted, Sunday turned out to be a glorious day. The temperature shot up to 24°C by ten o'clock, and the forecast said it would reach 32 by mid-afternoon. Mrs. Harper, with help from Hal and Tina, packed a picnic lunch while the other two went with Mr. Harper to gas up the car and pick up pop and ice. Amy called at ten-thirty to report that there was nothing to report, and by eleven they were on their way north to Pine Lake.

They invited Miss Gaynor to come with them, but she declined, saying that she should be on hand in case there was any news about Helen. Mrs. Harper offered to stay with her, but she wouldn't hear of it.

"I'll be just fine," she assured them. "I'm over the shock now and I want to start doing some checking on my own. Nick is coming over this afternoon, and we're going to plan our strategy."

* * *

"I don't know what that poor woman expects to do that the police haven't already done," Mrs. Harper commented as they were driving along.

"Maybe she thinks Nick has heard something that might provide a clue." Mr. Harper sounded unconvinced. "At any rate, it'll give her something to do."

"Boy, I wouldn't blame Helen if she'd just run off," Tina said. "Imagine having a father like that! He probably keeps her handcuffed to the bed at night."

"Oh, Tina!" her mother laughed. "I'm sure his bark is worse than his bite. He's no doubt very worried about his daughter, and that's why he sounded so gruff."

Tina looked doubtful, but she was soon distracted, along with the rest of the kids, by the search for the perfect picnic spot.

All in all, the day was a success. Hal took a

whole roll of film of everyone in various unflattering poses. "For my rogues gallery," he explained. "I think I'm going to be a people photographer. It's more interesting than scenery."

"You mean you're giving up taking pictures of paper towels and peanuts?" Tina laughed.

Hal ignored her and muttered, "Just you wait. When I've got a cover on *Life* then we'll see who laughs."

They arrived home a little after eight that evening to find Nick Gilbert sitting on the back patio with Helen's aunt.

"Wow!" Hal exclaimed when they had all be introduced. "Would it be okay if I took your picture? I'd sure like to have one of a bronc riding champ."

Nick's haunted look disappeared for a minute and he grinned at Hal. "Sure, why not?"

Hal let out a wild "Whoopee!" and ran into the house to reload his camera.

"Any word?" Mrs. Harper asked, sitting down next to Miss Gaynor.

"No, nothing. I called Arthur a little while ago, but he had nothing to report either."

"The police were over to talk to me early this afternoon," Nick said. "They think the kidnappers will likely be in contact before tomorrow. They said the best thing for us to do is just stay close to the phone and wait. But, boy, that's hard to do. When I think how terrified Helen must be right now—" he put his head in his hands—"and me sitting here doing nothing to help."

"Arthur wants to come here immediately," Miss Gaynor sighed. "I told him it's imperative that he stay home where the kidnappers can reach him. He said he would wait until tomorrow evening, then if he's had no word he'll come and take things into his own hands."

"Swell," Nick groaned. "That's all we need—Arthur Gaynor bungling the whole thing!"

At that moment Hal arrived clutching his camera and calling, "Okay everybody, cuddle up closer so I can get you all in."

After taking a couple of group shots, then a number of Nick alone, he handed the camera to Ted. "Take one of me and Nick together, okay?" he asked.

"Boy, wait'll the guys at home see this!" he cried when Ted was through. "I'll send you a print if it turns out good, Nick. Maybe if you as if it you'll let me be the official photographer at your wedding."

Nick's grin disappeared, and Miss Gaynor turned her head away.

"Oh, gee, I'm sorry." Hal looked as if he wished the patio would open up and swallow him.

"That's okay," Nick assured him with a wan smile. "And sure, you can take our wedding pictures—if there is a wedding."

"I think maybe you children had better get upstairs and have your showers. You've had a busy day and tomorrow will be even busier." Mrs. Harper stood up abruptly and led the way back into the house.

* * *

Monday morning the kids were up before seven. It was another perfect day and despite their concern, they were eager to get started.

"What's on for today?" Hal asked, sitting down at the breakfast table and helping himself to a piece of toast from Ted's plate.

"We don't have tickets for today's infield events," his aunt answered. "I thought you children might like to spend the day downtown. There's so much to see. We'll go to the infields tomorrow. Nick will be in his second go-round. Then we can take in the grandstand show in the evening."

"If you're ready in time you can drive down with me," Mr. Harper added.

"Sounds fine," Trish nodded. "I really should do some shopping."

Hal groaned and muttered, "Girls!"

"Do you want to come, Mom?" Tina asked ignoring him.

"No, I think I'd better stay here with Helen's aunt. She's putting on a good front, but underneath she's terribly frightened."

Tina nodded soberly and bent her head to her food. The whole business with Helen was putting a real pall over the week.

As though reading her mind, her mother said, "I want you children to put this whole tragic business out of your minds for today. There's nothing you can do to get Helen back, and I'm sure she wouldn't want your holiday spoiled because of her. The police are doing everything they can. She'll be found very soon."

Tina raised her head and smiled at her mother. She and the others would try, but it wasn't that easy.

* * *

They had watched the juggler, listened to a cowboy singing western songs, admired the various marching bands, joined the Stonies in a Native dance, and cheered on their favourites in the bar stool races. Now it was noon and the smells from a nearby hot dog stand were starting to get to them. They checked out the multitude of food kiosks, found one that didn't have too long a line and went in for lunch.

"So, what'll we do this aft?" Ted asked around a mouthful of hamburger.

"Tina and I are going shopping," Trish announced firmly.

"Well, I'm sure not going to spend all day in some dumb store," Hal said. "Let's you and me check out the action down at the other end of the mall, Ted."

"Okay," Ted agreed. "We'll meet you guys at, say . . ." He checked his watch. ". . . two-thirty. At the Bay."

"Fine." Trish wiped her mouth and stood up. "Ready, Tina?"

Tina gave her brother a long-suffering look and nodded.

As they were leaving Hal said to Ted, "Just one more burger and we're on our way, too."

The girls had checked out a few of the boutiques along the mall and were entering a drugstore when Tina's eye lit upon a woman dressed entirely in black—black dress, black shoes and stockings, black hat. The woman was stuffing things into a large bag slung across her shoulder: toothpaste, shampoo, deodorant. Tina grabbed Trish's arm and pointed. "Maybe I'm going crazy but I'm sure that's the old woman who's been watching Helen."

"How can you be sure?" Trish asked, moving toward a counter with demonstration perfume bottles along the top. "Those bag-ladies all look the same."

"Well, maybe," Tina agreed, craning her neck to get a better look.

The woman was reaching for a hairbrush when she suddenly seemed to become aware that she was being watched. She looked furtively around as she grabbed the brush and added it to the loot in her bag. Then she caught Tina's eye, pulled her bag quickly closed and rushed down the aisle to the exit. As she passed Tina and Trish, her face lost its furtive look and she stared at them with a mixture of fear and hate. The girls watched in stunned silence as she pushed her way through the door and grabbed hold of the grocery cart half-filled with pop cans that was standing just outside.

"She stole all that stuff!" Tina cried.

"Shouldn't we tell somebody?"

"Yeah, I guess we should. I'll see if I can find a clerk and you make sure she doesn't get away."

Tina nodded and hurried after the shoplifter.

By the time Tina got outside, the woman had the grocery cart firmly in her grip and was trying to fight her way through the crowd that had gathered to watch a street magician performing in the middle of the mall. Keeping an eye on the drugstore for Trish and a clerk to come out, Tina got as close to the woman as she could without letting her see she was being followed. The woman impatiently shoved the cart into the crowd, knocking a young girl over. The girl's mother turned and started to yell at the woman, who turned quickly aside, looking for an opening in the crowd. As she backed away a man coming in the opposite direction bumped into her, knocking her hat off.

Tina gasped. The woman's hair was tied at the back with an unusual plaid ribbon. The last time Tina had seen a ribbon like that was on the braid Helen had worn last Saturday.

CHAPTER 6

As Tina stared in shocked disbelief, the woman pushed her cart recklessly forward and disappeared into the crowd.

"Where did she go?" Trish cried, running up to Tina, a puzzled clerk from the drugstore not far behind.

"She just sort of got swallowed up by all these people," Tina answered, pushing her way through the crowd in the direction the woman seemed to have taken. "Come on, she can't have gone far."

But when the three managed to squeeze through the mass of people surrounding the magician and came out at the corner, there was no sign of the woman and her cart.

“Well, thanks anyway, girls,” the clerk smiled. “We’ll keep a watch out for her. If she tries any more shoplifting we’ll be ready.”

The clerk waved and began to fight his way back through the crowd.

“Gee, it’s too bad we—”

“Trish, listen,” Tina interrupted. “We’ve got to find a police officer.”

“But it’s time to meet the boys.”

“Well, okay, we’ll meet them, then go to the police station together. It’s not very far away.”

“Hey, wait a minute.” Trish grabbed her arm to stop her from tearing off down the street. “It’s not our responsibility to report her to the cops. The people in the drugstore will do that.”

“I know that,” Tina cried, shrugging out of Trish’s grasp. “It’s not the shoplifting we have to tell the police about. It’s the ribbon.”

“What ribbon? Hey, Tina, do you think maybe you got too much sun yesterday?”

“Trish, this isn’t funny. That woman was wearing Helen’s ribbon. I think the police should question her about where she got it. I bet she knows where Helen is!”

“Oh, wow!” Trish’s eyes opened wide. “Are you sure?”

"Sure I'm sure. The ribbon is very unusual. It's just too much of a coincidence that the old woman would have one exactly like it. Now come on, we haven't got a minute to lose."

Tina pushed her way down the two blocks to the Bay corner with Trish in her new cowboy boots struggling valiantly to keep up. When they arrived at the meeting place, Ted and Hal were already there.

Tina wasted no time bringing the boys up to date on what had been happening. Ted was less than enthusiastic about Tina's detective work, and Hal was downright scornful.

"Come on, Tina," Hal laughed, "you can't be serious. The cops'll laugh you right out of the station."

"Okay, if that's how you feel, Trish and I will go there alone."

"No," Ted shook his head, "we'll come with you. But I honestly don't think you've got much to go on."

Tina gave her brother a grateful look. "That's where you're wrong, Ted. Okay, let's get moving."

* * *

"Whoa! Hold on there, little lady." The

desk sergeant held up his hand and smiled down at Tina. "Now take it slow. Who is this woman you think is involved in the Helen Gaynor case? And how do you know Helen's missing, anyway? It hasn't been in the papers."

Tina took a deep breath and started again. "My sister is one of the princesses. Helen's aunt is staying with us. We know all about how Helen was lured away from the nursing home last Saturday."

The sergeant nodded. "Okay, go on. Tell me about the woman."

"Well, she always wears the same clothes; all black. We saw her watching Helen at the parade and again when the girls were being interviewed at Rope Square. Then today she was lifting stuff from a drugstore. We tried to catch her but she got away in the crowd."

"Is that all?"

"No. See, Helen wore a green and gold ribbon on her braid. It is very unusual—plaid and kind of glittery. Well, when I was chasing the woman in black, her hat came off and I saw she was wearing Helen's ribbon."

The sergeant was making a few notes on a pad and obviously trying hard not to smile.

"Anything else about this woman that might help us identify her?"

"Yes," Tina replied. "She has this grocery cart with her all the time. She collects stuff, mostly soft drink cans."

The sergeant put his head back and roared. "Oh, for Pete's sake, you must mean Pop Can Polly. She's a real character. Been around these parts for almost a year now." He gave another chuckle and blew his nose. "But she's perfectly harmless, I can assure you, miss. Doesn't bother anybody; keeps to herself. A pretty pathetic sort of character."

"She can't be all that harmless if she steals from stores," Trish put in.

"That seems hard to believe. This is the first time I've heard of her doing anything illegal. She tries real hard to keep on the good side of the police so we won't hassle her about scavenging, I guess. However, you may be right. We'll check into it. But as far as being involved with your friend, I'm afraid that's pretty farfetched."

"What about the ribbon?" Tina demanded.

"Well, now, we can't pull her in because she's wearing a funny ribbon. Likely it's not as uncommon as you think."

"It's Helen's ribbon. I *know* it! That woman must have been involved in the kidnapping somehow." Tina's voice was getting higher and more emotional. "You've just *got* to do something!"

The sergeant was obviously getting a little impatient. He shut his notepad and frowned.

"Cool it, Tina," Ted whispered. Then to the sergeant: "Thanks for your time, sir. We'll be going now."

The sergeant's frown disappeared, and he nodded pleasantly. "We'll keep an eye on Polly. If she's started shoplifting, we'll put a stop to it. Thanks for coming in."

He walked over to the door, obviously expecting them to follow. Tina opened her mouth to try one more time, but Ted and Hal didn't give her a chance. One on either side, they hustled her through the door before she could cause any more embarrassment.

"I don't care what you or that dumb sergeant say. I'm *sure* that woman knows something about Helen." The kids were walking back toward the middle of town. "I've always thought there was something very peculiar about the way she watched her. She's mixed up in this kidnapping somehow. I just *know* it."

"You really should try to break your Agatha Christie habit, Tina," Ted laughed. "I'm afraid it's getting to you. Do you honestly think that just because you saw

Polly watching Helen a couple of times and thought she was wearing a ribbon like Helen's that she's automatically guilty?''

"Yeah, face it, Tina,'' Hal said. "The sergeant was right. Anybody could be wearing a ribbon like Helen's. Now, come on. I think I see an ice cream stand in the next block.''

Tina had no choice but to drop the whole thing. Nobody believed her; maybe she was being foolish. Yet, there was something the sergeant had said in the station that had rung a bell. She hadn't stopped to figure it out, and now she couldn't remember what it was. But something hadn't quite fit.

They arrived at the ice cream stand and ordered cones. While the rest of the kids sat in the shade of a tree gobbling their ice cream and arguing about what they would do with the rest of the afternoon, Tina stood apart, trying to reconstruct the conversation at the police station. There had been something, all right, but try as she might she couldn't come up with it.

"Hey, Tina, wake up and join the party,'' Hal called to her. "We're going to the Glenbow Museum.''

Tina gave up the mental exercise and joined them. The best thing to do was stop thinking about it; it would come to her in time. At least she hoped it *would* be in time.

CHAPTER 7

When the kids got home after spending a fasçinating afternoon in the museum they found Mrs. Harper entertaining a tall, burly man dressed in traditional Western clothing: worn but expensive cowboy boots, leather jacket, plaid shirt and fringed vest. He looked about forty-five years old and would have been very good looking if it weren't for the scowl on his face.

As the group stood at the doors to the patio where the two were sitting, Mrs. Harper rose and beckoned them to come forward.

"This is Helen's father, children," she said, her usually cheerful face clouded over. "Mr. Gaynor—my son and daughter and their cousins."

The kids smiled politely at Mr. Gaynor then looked inquisitively at Mrs. Harper.

"Mr. Gaynor is here to investigate Helen's disappearance," she said in answer to their unspoken question.

"But I thought the cops said—"

Hal didn't get a chance to finish. Mr. Gaynor's booming voice interrupted him. "Incompetent bunch of nincompoops. Couldn't find their butt with both hands. I know. I've had dealings with the law before." His ruddy face turned even redder and he gave a loud snort.

"Where's Miss Gaynor?" Tina asked hesitant.

"She's upstairs lying down. I'm afraid it's been a very hard day for her."

"I'll bet it has!" Ted whispered to Tina, glancing with distaste at Helen's father.

"Yes, Charlotte does a lot of that," Mr. Gaynor sneered. "Probably that's what she was doing when Helen was kidnapped."

"Oh, really, I don't think Miss Gaynor can be blamed for the kidnapping," Mrs. Harper responded. "As I understand it, Helen slipped away without anyone knowing about it."

"Hmph! Well, maybe so. I still think she's

run off with that drugstore cowboy from the next farm—Nick Gilbert, big rodeo star. Or so Helen was led to believe. Nothing but a—"

"Did someone mention my name?" Nick Gilbert asked as he rounded the side of the house.

When he walked up the steps to the patio, the air around the table became charged. Helen's father half rose from his seat, and the two men stared at one another.

"What the devil are *you* doing here?" Mr. Gaynor demanded.

"I've come to see Helen's aunt. What are *you* doing here? I thought the police told you to stay home and wait for word from the kidnappers—a ransom note or something."

"There's been no ransom note, and I don't expect one. You've got Helen stashed away somewhere just waiting for a chance to take off with her. Figure you'll win enough at the rodeo to pull it off, do you, big shot?"

"Don't be a complete fool. Helen's been kidnapped. Can't you get that through your head?"

The angry bluster seemed to drain out of the man right in front of their eyes. He slumped back into his chair and rested his head in his hands.

Nick took a chair across from him and

turned his head away, obviously trying to get hold of himself.

"It seems to me that a good deal more could be accomplished if we all co-operated rather than accused one another," Mrs. Harper reasoned. "The police are doing everything they can. I'm sure they'll have good news for us soon."

No one answered her, and as the silence became uncomfortable Tina spoke up. "I saw a woman today wearing a ribbon that looked just like Helen's."

Ted groaned and Hal muttered, "Oh, no!"

Nick turned quickly around and stared at Tina. "A ribbon like Helen's? What do you mean?"

"Well, Helen wore this really unusual ribbon on her braid. It was glittery gold and green in a funny pattern."

"I know the one you mean. I gave it to her when she won the Stampede Queen contest. A friend of mine who's into weaving made it for me."

"See?" Tina was triumphant. "I told you I was right about the ribbon. It *is* unique."

"Maybe the old dame saw Helen get kidnapped," Hal said. "How else could she have gotten hold of the ribbon?"

"More likely she found it where it came off

Helen's braid," Ted answered. "It could have been anywhere."

"Or she could have taken Helen herself," Tina said, but no one was paying any attention to her.

Nick was on his feet and heading into the house, followed quickly by Helen's father.

"Where are you going?" Mrs. Harper cried.

"Got to find that woman," Mr. Gaynor answered.

"To talk to the police," Nick said at the same time.

* * *

Nick apparently had more luck with the police than Tina had. He phoned Helen's aunt just as the family and their guests were sitting down to a late dinner.

"He was able to convince the authorities that the ribbon Tina saw almost certainly came from Helen's braid," Miss Gaynor reported. "They have all their units on the lookout for the woman they call Pop Can Polly. It shouldn't be long before they pick her up." For the first time since she'd come to stay with the Harpers she looked positively cheerful.

"That's wonderful!" Mrs. Harper cried. "Tina, you should be proud of yourself for being so observant."

Tina beamed and the other three nodded uncomfortably.

Mr. Gaynor had declined Mrs. Harper's offer to put him up, explaining that he had taken a room at the Westin Hotel. They hadn't heard from him since he had stormed out of the house that afternoon determined to find Polly on his own.

"I'll call Arthur right now and give him the good news," Miss Gaynor continued.

"Ask him if he'd like to join us for dinner," Mrs. Harper suggested.

When she came back from the phone Helen's aunt was looking concerned.

"He's not at his hotel. They haven't seen him since he checked in this morning."

"I guess he's still out looking for Polly," Ted suggested.

"I don't see how he expects to do that," Tina argued. "He has no idea what she looks like. It doesn't make any sense."

"It does seem odd," her father mused. "However, I suppose the man is beside himself with worry and feels he has to be doing *something*."

"I suppose so," Tina answered uncertainly.

Dinner went ahead without any more discussion of the case. When the meal was over, Mrs. Harper suggested the kids head straight for bed.

"It's going to be a long day tomorrow; the grandstand show doesn't finish till well after ten."

"But we want to stay up in case there's some news from the police," Hal pleaded.

"If there's any news I promise we'll wake you and tell you," his uncle smiled.

But they didn't hear anything more until early the next morning. Nick brought the news himself.

He had apparently spent the night around the police station waiting for some word on Polly. Finally at about seven-thirty in the morning, a patrol car picked her up and brought her to the station.

"They kept her for an hour trying to get some fix on where she found the ribbon," Nick told the eager group in the Harpers' living room, "but it was hopeless. She insisted she couldn't remember. She picks up stuff all over the city, raids garbage cans. She could have found it anywhere."

"It *was* Helen's ribbon, though, wasn't it?" Trish asked.

"Oh, yes. I identified it for the police.

There was no mistaking it."

Miss Gaynor slumped back in her chair. The forlorn, helpless look had returned.

"I guess I'll have to try to get hold of Arthur," she sighed. "I can't understand why he doesn't call."

She rose reluctantly from the chair and headed for the telephone in the kitchen.

"One positive thing happened at the station," Nick told the group when Miss Gaynor had left the room. "There was a reporter there from the *Herald* when they brought Polly in. He managed to get the story of Helen's disappearance, so it will be in the papers tomorrow. It might help us find Helen."

"Did the reporter talk to you, Nick?" Hal asked eagerly.

"Yeah. Even took my picture—'the stricken fiance.' You know the kind of human interest stuff newspapers love."

Just then Miss Gaynor came back and the newspaper article was forgotten.

"Did you get hold of him?" Mrs. Harper asked.

"Yes, he was in his room. I passed on the bad news about Polly and the ribbon. Of course, he didn't believe a word of it. Says the police don't know what they're doing.

He's still determined to find her himself and talk to her."

"Oh, great!" Nick laughed. "He'll probably get arrested for harassment. But at least he won't be around here bothering you people."

"What if he does find Polly? What do you think he'll do?" Tina asked.

"Knowing Arthur Gaynor he'll probably try to bully her," Nick answered. "But quite honestly I don't think he will find her. It took the police over twelve hours and they have all the resources. It would certainly be best for everyone if he didn't."

But that's where he was dead wrong.

CHAPTER 8

Mrs. Harper insisted that the bad news Nick brought should not stop the kids from having a full, exciting day. There was nothing they could do to bring Helen back, and worrying certainly wouldn't help.

"So get your stuff together and let's be on our way," she said, moving toward the door and motioning the children to follow.

"But we haven't had breakfast yet!" Hal wailed.

"Don't worry, Hal," his aunt smiled. "We're going to have a real Western breakfast at the Chinook Mall. Can you join us, Nick?" She turned to the tall, worried-looking young man standing beside Helen's aunt.

"And what about you, Miss Gaynor? I think getting away for a while would do you a world of good."

Nick shook his head. "Sorry, Ma'am, I'd love to. But I'm riding in my second go-round this afternoon and I haven't had any sleep since Sunday night. I suppose I'd better hit the sack for a few hours if I expect to do well enough to qualify for the finals. But, Charlotte, why don't you go with them? There's really nothing you can do here."

"I suppose you're right, Nick," Helen's aunt sighed. "But I don't really feel right about going off and enjoying myself when goodness knows what Helen is—" She broke off and brought her handkerchief up to her eyes.

"Come," Mrs. Harper soothed. "It will do you good. And we'll come back to the house as soon as we've had breakfast and driven the children over to Stampede Park."

Charlotte nodded reluctantly and rose to follow the rest out of the room.

Fifteen minutes later Mrs. Harper, Miss Gaynor and the kids were piling out of the station wagon at the huge mall on the south side of the city. Music from a Western band filled the air and the smell of frying bacon and hot coffee made the group feel as if they were truly in cowboy country.

They followed Mrs. Harper down the aisle of cars to the long table in front of the mall proper where the delicious smells were coming from. As they stood in line waiting for their plate of pancakes and bacon, an old time fiddler and a caller stepped up to the mike and a group of fancy-dressed square dancers began to whirl and turn.

Everyone watched the dancers and clapped in time to the music. Everyone, that is, except Hal who was frantically trying to focus his camera while keeping his place in the food line-up.

Eventually the group, plates of food and cups of coffee in hand, found themselves a shady spot in which to eat.

"Tell us more about Helen's father, Miss Gaynor," Ted asked when they had finished eating and were relaxing, listening to the music.

"My brother was always strong-willed," Miss Gaynor began after a moment. "He met Angela, Helen's mother, at the 1967 Stampede. He was competing in the rodeo and Helen's mother was one of the princesses. They had a whirlwind courtship and were married just two weeks later. Angela had no family. Her mother and father had died in a car accident a couple of years earlier, and I think the idea of an older man to take care of her was very appealing. Arthur took her back to his ranch near Cochrane, and a couple of years later Helen was born. I was nursing in Florida at the time but I managed the occasional visit. The first time I saw them they were ecstatically happy. Then the next time, which was a few years later—Helen was just a toddler—Angela seemed to have changed. All the old sparkle had gone and she had aged ten years. I wasn't back to Canada again until almost three years later after Angela had died."

"That's really sad," Tina cried. "Was Mr. Gaynor pretty broken up?"

"It was very hard to tell. He wouldn't talk about it; wouldn't talk about hardly anything except the ranch, for that matter. He became very withdrawn—almost cold—except when he was with little Helen. He was the warmest, most loving father you could imagine. Then when Helen grew up and began to get interested in boys he retreated into his cold shell again and became the strict, almost cruel person you saw yesterday. Her interest in Nick Gilbert just about put him over the edge."

"Did he really forbid Helen to see Nick?"

Trish asked, her eyes as big a banjoes.

"As much as he could, but Helen herself inherited his strong will. She managed to see Nick and to get engaged to him in spite of her father's disapproval." She paused a moment and seemed to be searching for the right word. "I don't think Arthur really disapproves of Nick as a person," she continued. "It's just that he doesn't want Helen to get involved with anyone. He wants to keep her all to himself."

"My goodness, that sounds like something right out of the last century," Mrs. Harper exclaimed.

"Poor Helen," Trish sighed. "If I was her, I'd run away and he'd never find me."

"That's exactly what was going through my mind," Miss Gaynor murmured.

* * *

Mrs. Harper drove the kids to the grounds, dropped them at the south gate with their tickets and told them she and Uncle George would meet them at six-thirty under the tower clock.

"Have a wonderful time," she called as she put the car in gear, "and root hard for Nick."

The infield events started at one-thirty and by one-fifteen the kids were in the stands, fortified with candy floss, hot dogs and soft drinks.

"There are nine events before the saddle bronc riding," Ted noted, peering at his program. "And Nick is riding fourth. He's got a two point lead on the guy that's second so he should qualify for the finals unless he really blows it."

"I dunno," Tina frowned, "he sure looked tired this morning, and like he didn't care much if he won or lost."

"Sure he cares," Hal countered full of indignation. "He's a pro."

At that moment the band struck up a rousing Western tune and from behind the far bleachers ten girls on horseback, each carrying a provincial flag, rode into the infield. Following them were Amy and Rhonda. The afternoon performance had begun.

The kids, having seen one afternoon of competition, regarded themselves as seasoned rodeo experts. They watched the buffalo riding and the wild cow milking with a critical eye, then cheered for their favourite in the bareback bronc riding, a tall lanky cowboy who had been bucked off the first go-round.

When the rodeo clowns came on, they laughed at the clever antics they used to divert the wild animals away from the riders who had been thrown. Finally, after the boys' steer riding competition and another exchange between the main clown and the announcer, the saddle bronc riding began.

Rhythm is the key in this event, the program explained. The rider spurs from the horse's neck in a full swing toward the back of the saddle in time with the bronc's action. To qualify, the rider must have his spurs over the break of the horse's shoulders until the horse completes his first jump out of the chute. A rider is disqualified if he touches any part of the horse or his equipment with his free hand, loses a stirrup or is bucked off before he has been riding for eight seconds. He gains points for reaching the full length of the arc with his toes turned outward.

The first rider was bucked off before the eight-second horn sounded, and the second and third did only moderately well, scoring a 69 and a 71. Then Nick burst out of the chute.

When they had seen him ride the first time, he had thrilled them with his ease and grace in the saddle, moving almost as one with his horse. This time, however, he was a different person. His movements were jerky and he barely made the eight-second limit before being bucked off.

"Nick Gilbert: 71." The announcement sent a ripple of concern through the group.

"Does that mean he's out of the running?" Trish asked.

"Not necessarily," Ted answered. "He has a two day total of 150. He could still make it unless too many riders do a lot better."

They watched the next seven riders anxiously, hoping at least some of them would get bucked off or make a bad showing. The best score was a low 75.

"That's good, isn't it?" Trish asked. "Nick's only four points behind the winner."

"Yes, but remember he's competing with all the riders still to come," Ted explained. "Let's just hope there aren't fourteen riders with better scores."

Although the rest of the events were equally as exciting as the saddle bronc riding, they were an anti-climax to the kids. They stayed for the steer wrestling and the wild horse race, then as the next event was about to start —the calf roping contest—Trish announced that she was leaving.

"I can't bear to see those poor little calves being dragged along the ground," she said.

"I'm going to get a drink, then go look at some of the exhibits."

Tina, who wasn't any happier about the calf roping than Trish, decided to go with her. The boys said they would stay till the end, then meet the girls at the agriculture building at about four-thirty. "Yuck!" Trish groaned, twitching her nose. "That place smells awful."

"We'll be there," Tina declared, ignoring her cousin's reaction. "Trish can always wait outside if the smell gets too much for her."

The girls left the grandstand and headed for the midway.

"Hey, let's take one of those little cars that travel up above the crowds," Tina suggested. "We can get on right over there." She pointed to a stand where a man was selling tickets and another was helping people into small cable cars.

"Well, I don't know," Trish hesitated. "I'm not that crazy about heights."

"Oh, don't be a dope. It's loads of fun. You get a bird's-eye view of everything in the park."

She took her cousin's arm and pulled her along to the booth.

"Now, aren't you glad you came?" Tina asked as she peered over the edge of the cable car at the crowd below. "You can see absolutely everything."

Trish was sitting rigidly in her seat with her eyes closed and her hands gripping the bar.

"Yeah, it's swell," she muttered.

Tina looked over at her and started to laugh. Then she stopped abruptly. Out of the corner of her eye she had caught sight of a familiar figure pushing a grocery cart half full of pop cans.

"Trish!" she cried. "There's Polly. Gosh, she really gets around, doesn't she?"

She watched the woman in black stop and pick through a garbage can, retrieving half a dozen cans and tossing them into her cart. As the cable car continued toward the north end of the Park, Tina kept her eye on Polly as she pushed her cart along, stopping every now and then to pick up a discarded can.

By the time she had passed from view, Tina felt uneasy. There was something wrong with what she had just seen, but she couldn't for the life of her figure out what. It was like the business at the police station. Something there didn't quite fit either, but she had never been able to come up with what it was.

The car gradually came to a stop at the end of the line and the girls got off—Trish with white knuckles and Tina with a worried frown. They started toward the front entrance to the Roundup Centre and were just about to go in when Tina stopped dead in her tracks and grabbed Trish's arm.

"Trish, I've just remembered." She stood for a moment, eyes half closed, thinking. Then she turned and started running back the way they had come.

Trish's mouth dropped open. Then she hurried to catch up with her cousin. "What on earth has got into you, Tina?" she panted from a few paces behind.

"Hurry, Trish. We've got to find her and follow her."

"Find who?"

"Pop Can Polly. I just remembered something. If I'm not mistaken, she'll lead us to Helen."

CHAPTER 9

"What do you mean? What did you remember?" Trish had finally caught up to Tina, who had slowed down and was peering through the crowd.

"It's her grocery cart," Tina answered. "She always has the cans she collects loose in the cart. But remember the day Helen disappeared? The cart was covered by a tarp. Quick, she's heading out through the gates."

"I think you've really flipped this time, Tina," Trish gasped, struggling to keep up. "What's a tarpaulin got to do with anything?"

"Don't you see? When we saw Polly pushing the grocery cart that day we thought she had pop cans under the tarp. But she's never covered them up before; she just throws them in. So what do you suppose the tarp was for?"

"You mean . . . ?"

"I think she could have had Helen in that cart. You know how tiny Helen is. She could have been curled up under that tarp and no one would have known it. And the timing is right. Helen disappeared sometime after four-thirty, and we saw Polly about five-thirty. That would have given her just enough time to kidnap Helen and bring her downtown where we saw her."

"That's the most ridiculous thing I've ever heard!" Trish laughed. "Is that *all* you've got to go on?"

"No, it's not. I finally remembered what didn't fit down at the police station. Remember the sergeant said that Polly never broke the law? That she had to keep on the good side of the cops? So why was she breaking it when we saw her in the drugstore? And what was she lifting?"

"Toothpaste, comb, soap, deodorant," Trish answered. "So what?"

"Why would she suddenly need toothpaste and deodorant and pretty soap so desperately that she'd steal it?"

"Oh, I *see*!" Trish gasped. "But why on earth would she want to kidnap Helen? If it was for money, why hasn't she tried to get in touch with anyone?"

"How should I know? Maybe she just likes pretty things."

"Tina, don't joke. This is serious."

"I'm not joking. I read a book of Mom's once about this guy who kidnapped a girl and kept her in his basement just so he could look at her. He also collected butterflies and mounted them. Needless to say he was nuts."

"And you think Pop Can Polly is nuts?"

"Don't you? Anyway, all I can say is that it suddenly fits together: her watching Helen with that half-crazy look and then stealing stuff that she obviously doesn't use herself. And it's not so far-fetched to think of her luring Helen away from the rest of the people at the nursing home, grabbing her when she wasn't looking and somehow knocking her out, then taking her away in the grocery cart. After all, Helen's real tiny and Polly looks pretty strong."

"But you still haven't explained—"

"Oh, rats!" Tina interrupted. "We've lost her in that crowd. Come on, hurry. We might still catch up with her."

"How do you know which way she went?"

"I'm not sure," Tina called over her shoulder, "but I figure she must live quite near that restaurant where we ate the day Helen was kidnapped. Remember how she was there one minute, then the next she'd disappeared?"

The girls ran through the gates and turned west on Seventeenth Avenue. The sidewalks were crowded, and it was almost impossible to see more than half a block ahead. They crossed Macleod Trail and were heading for First Street East when the crowds thinned out a little and Tina spotted the black-clad figure hurrying along a block ahead of them.

"I was right. She *did* head this way."

Two blocks later they lost her. A gang of young people came out of a restaurant and blocked the sidewalk. By the time Tina and Trish managed to push their way through, there was no sign of Polly.

"Darn anyway!" Tina cried. "She's gone."

"There's the restaurant where we ate the other day," Trish pointed out. "Do you think she went into one of those buildings? Some of them look pretty run down."

"There's no way to tell," Tina sighed. "We can poke around a little bit, I guess."

They crossed the street and, passing the

restaurant, walked down to the entrance to an alley.

"I'll bet she turned in here," Tina said, as she peered cautiously around the corner of an old building. "That would explain her disappearing so quickly the other day. Come on, let's see what's down here."

Moving as quietly as possible they began to edge their way down the dark alley. It appeared to be empty except for a scraggly grey cat which shot out from between the two buildings ahead of them and caused Trish to let out of blood-curdling shriek.

"Shush, for Pete's sake!" Tina cautioned. "She may be anywhere around here."

They crept past the space where the cat had been and came to a dark doorway.

"I wonder if this is where she lives," Tina whispered, as the two girls examined the rickety door. "I think it's op—" Suddenly she heard a noise behind her. She whirled around and standing almost on top of them was the woman in black.

CHAPTER 10

"What are you two doing snooping around here?" She reached out and grabbed each of the girls by the shoulder. Then with her foot she kicked the door open and shoved Trish and Tina through it. They landed in a heap on the floor, and before either of them could react, Polly slammed the door. They heard a key turning in a lock and then there was total silence.

Instinctively, the girls edged into a corner and huddled together in the darkness, hardly daring to breathe. They heard the woman moving around across from them, but could not see her. Then a crack of light appeared as an inner door opened, and they could see her slip through.

They waited without moving for what seemed hours, then the door opened again and Polly reappeared. They heard her lock the door, then she brushed past them in the darkness. The exit opened and Polly slipped through into the alley.

Another eternity passed before Tina finally stood up and began to feel her way across the room.

"It seems to be a sort of vestibule," she said as she felt along the walls. "There's a coat rack and a shelf above it."

"It smells awful," Trish whimpered. "And it's so hot. Oh, Tina, what are we going to do?"

"Here's the door," Tina said ignoring Trish's wailing. "Maybe if we both push against it we can force it open. Come on, Trish, I need you."

Trish got up and followed Tina's voice until she was beside her in front of the outside door.

"Okay—one, two, three, PUSH!" They threw their full weight against the door, but it refused to budge. Three more times they flung themselves against the wooden barrier, still with no success.

"Okay, let's try the other one, the one the

woman went through. Maybe it's not so strong." Tina took Trish's hand and they moved cautiously through the blackness of the small room.

"Same drill," Tina ordered. "Push after three." On the first try nothing happened, but on the second there was a distinct splitting sound.

"I think it's giving," Trish cried. Sure enough, the third effort tore the top hinge away from the frame. Two more strong pushes and the door gave way completely. The girls staggered forward into a large dimly lit room and looked dazedly around.

"My gosh! Look at all this old stuff!" Tina exclaimed. "There must be half a dozen couches to say nothing of all the chairs and tables. What do you suppose it is?"

"Maybe somebody's extra storage space. The electricity is still running." She pointed to a naked bulb swinging above their heads. "Polly is probably just borrowing it, hoping the owners don't use it much."

The girls began to weave their way through the dusty, foul-smelling furniture. Ahead of them were two doors, both shut.

"Oh, please, let one of them lead outside," Trish pleaded. The first door, however, opened onto a dilapidated kitchen, its rusty stove and corroded sink looking as if they hadn't been used since before the first Stampede. A mouse, frightened by the noise, scrambled over Trish's foot in a mad dash out the door. Tina clamped her hand over her cousin's mouth before she could scream, and pulled her quickly out of the doorway.

They approached the second door and Tina tried the knob.

"It's locked," she reported with a sigh.

Trish, still slightly addled by her encounter with the mouse, said, "Come on, we'll break it down like we did the other one. I can't stay here another minute." And she began throwing her shoulder into the door.

The wood was strong and resisted her effort. As she reeled backwards from the impact a voice came from the other side. "Who's there?"

"Did you hear that?" Trish turned wide-eyed to Tina.

"Someone's in there," Tina answered in a low voice. Then she called out, "Can you open the door from your side?"

"No, I can't," came the desperate reply. "Oh, please, whoever you are, help me!"

"Hang on! We'll keep trying. If only the door weren't so thick." She looked frantically around the room.

"Please hurry—before she comes back."

"Come on, Trish, we'll never break this door down. We've got to find something to force the lock." Tina ran back to the kitchen.

"I hope you don't expect me to go back in that horrid room," Trish called after her.

"Never mind, I'll find something myself." She disappeared behind the first door and a moment later came out carrying a large carving knife.

"If we can just get this between the door and the jamb, I think we can jimmy the lock," Tina said as she came toward Trish. Working in silence for a minute or two, she managed to wedge the knife into the small space. "Okay, now push." The two girls gripped the knife handle between them and shoved with all their might. For a moment, nothing happened. Then with a tremendous crack, the door flew open. Tina dropped the knife in her surprise, and both girls fell into a brightly lit bedroom.

In contrast to the rest of the hovel the room was clean and airy. The furniture was old, but the dust and cobwebs had been swept away and the cracked linoleum floor was shining.

They looked around in awe, then their gaze fell on the bed. It stood in the far corner of the room, half-hidden under an elaborate, satin canopy. And on it, her ankle attached by a long chain to the footboard, sat a young woman.

"Helen! It *is* you!" Tina cried, rushing over to her.

"Oh, am I glad to see you kids," Helen Gaynor sobbed.

"What happened?" Trish gasped.

"There's no time to explain now. She could be back any minute. Please, run and get help."

"But we can't leave you here like this, Helen," Tina said worriedly. "If that woman comes back and finds us gone she'll know we'll be bringing the police and she'll just take you someplace else."

"Maybe we could cut through the chain with the knife," Trish suggested. "It doesn't look that strong."

"Good idea," Tina answered, rushing back to where she'd dropped the knife.

While the girls worked on the chain, Helen began to explain what had happened to her.

"I got this call to come to the hospital, that my boyfriend had been hurt. We were just a couple of blocks away, so I ran straight out of the nursing home to go to him. I'd only gone about half a block when this woman stepped out from behind a clump of bushes and grabbed me. I tried to struggle, but she put a cloth over my face, and the next thing I knew I woke up here on this bed. I don't even know what day it is."

"It's Tuesday. You've been here three days." Tina barely looked up from sawing on the chain. She was working so hard her arms were beginning to ache. "Okay," she said at last, "I think this link is beginning to wear through. Just another couple of minutes and we'll have you free."

"Oh, thank heavens!" The tears began to pour down Helen's face. "I don't know what I would have done if you hadn't come along." She paused for a moment, a startled look passing across her face. "But who are you and why on earth *did* you come along?"

"This is Trish Jacobs and I'm Tina Harper, Amy's sister. We've been trying to figure out where you were ever since you disappeared. Finally, we followed the woman in black."

Trish picked up the story, "Tina figured out that she must have kidnapped you. We lost sight of her, then came down the alley behind the building looking for her."

"But she found us first and locked us in a tiny room just inside the door," Tina added, still hacking at the chain. "There!" She gave a jerk and the chain parted. "You'll have to walk with the chain on your ankle, but at least you can walk. Come on. Let's get out of here. Does that door lead outside?" She pointed to a small door a few feet from the bed.

"No, that's the bathroom. Fortunately,the chain was long enough for me to reach it. I tried to find something to break the chain with, but she was too smart to leave anything around." She shook her head dazedly. "You're really Amy's sister? It's all very confusing."

"I suppose it is. But we haven't time to go into detail now. We're going to have to go back the way we came," Tina said, helping Helen up from the bed.

"But how are we going to get out the back door?" Trish wailed. "We tried to force it before, remember, and it didn't budge."

"We'll break the lock with the knife, the same as we did here. With three of us forcing it we shouldn't have too much trouble."

But when Tina shoved the knife blade in between the door and the jamb and all three began to push on the handle, nothing happened. The door might have been made of solid steel for all the impression they were making.

"It's no use," Helen said. "We're only going to break the knife." She slumped against the wall and sighed.

"Aren't there any windows?" Trish asked.

"I didn't see any," Tina answered. "This seems to be the only way out."

"Look," Trish suddenly brightened. "The old woman's going to come back sometime, right?"

The other two nodded.

"Well, then, we'll be ready for her. When she comes through the door we'll threaten her with the knife, then escape."

"Trish, this isn't *Nancy Drew*," Tina sniffed.

"Have you got a better idea?"

Tina thought for a minute. "Maybe we could rig up something to trip her when she comes in the door."

"Yeah, and just how would we do that?" Trish countered, a little annoyed at Tina's abrupt dismissal of her idea. "It would take forever to find a rope and hammer and nails. By that time the old woman would likely be back."

"She's right, Tina," Helen said. "We have to think of something fast. Maybe the knife idea is our best bet. At least it's worth a try."

"Okay, who's going to do the bit with the knife? Not me, that's for sure." Tina shook her head emphatically.

"I'll do it," Helen offered. "After what she put me through, it will be a pleasure."

"Was she really mean to you?" Trish breathed. "Did she beat you or torture you or stuff like that?"

Helen gave her a weak smile. "No, nothing like that. Actually, she was very kind to me; brought me a comb and shampoo, and fed me pretty good deli food, too. But she *did* keep me chained to a bed, not knowing from one minute to the next if she would suddenly go completely off the deep end and kill me. It wasn't exactly a lot of fun."

"Well, it's nearly over now," Trish said. "Nick will be so happy to see you."

"You've met Nick?" Helen asked.

"Sure. He's been nearly crazy ever since you disappeared." Tina brought Helen up to up to date on what had happened since she'd been kidnapped by Pop Can Polly.

"And your father was determined to find Polly himself and wring the truth out of her," Tina finished.

"That's Daddy, all right," Helen sighed. "I suppose he and Nick got into one of their usual fights."

"I guess it wasn't exactly a fight," Tina answered. "I think your father—"

"Hush!" Helen whispered suddenly. "I think I hear someone at the door." She grabbed the knife firmly in her right hand and gestured for the girls to get behind her.

They held their breath as a key turned in the lock and the door was thrown open. Helen held the knife in front of her, pointing it at Polly as she backed into the vestibule.

"Get in here and close the door," she ordered in a shaky voice. "I've got a knife."

Polly swung around, pulling the grocery cart with her. "Give me that knife!" she ordered, reaching out her hand and moving toward Helen.

"Don't come any closer. Please. Don't make me have to use this thing." Helen's voice was barely audible.

The woman moved forward. The knife began to shake in Helen's hand. For one long moment the woman and the girl stood motionless staring at one another. Finally, Helen's arm dropped and the knife clattered to the floor.

"I can't do it!" she said softly. "I just can't do it!"

Tina and Trish watched in confusion and terror. Why couldn't Helen at least have hung onto the knife? Both girls dived for it—a split second too late. Polly had grabbed it and was gesturing towards them.

"I *knew* you'd be trouble from the day I saw you in the drugstore," she snarled, waving the knife in the air. "Now get in there before I have to use this thing."

Helen and the girls slumped dejectedly back through the filthy room and into the bedroom. As they stood huddled together, Polly grabbed a long cord hanging from the canopy over the bed and pulled it down.

"All right," she ordered, cutting the cord in half and tossing the pieces to Helen, "start tying their wrists to the bed posts. And make sure the knots are strong."

Helen had no choice but to do as she was told.

When the girls were secured to the old woman's satisfaction she turned to Helen and said, "Now for you." She reached into her black bag, took out a bottle and wadded up a handkerchief. Then she shook some of the bottle's contents onto the cloth. In a flash she had Helen by the hair and was pressing the cloth to her face. Seconds later Helen slumped to the floor.

Tina and Trish watched in growing panic as Polly hauled an old canvas bag out from under the bed and began to force Helen inside.

"What are you doing?" Tina cried.

"I'm taking her away where no one will find her," Polly replied. "She'll be with me forever." She grinned wickedly. "Nobody but me will ever see her by the falls." She slung the canvas bag over her shoulder and turned toward the door.

"Don't worry," she called without looking back, "I'll phone the police and tell them where you are when we're safely out of town. At least, I will if I remember." She let out a high-pitched giggle and slammed the door.

CHAPTER 11

The final event, the bull riding championships, was over. The boys, attempting to beat the crowd, slipped down the aisle and out of the grandstand a few minutes past four-thirty.

"Wait a sec, Ted," Hal called, stopping to focus his camera on the impressive finale that was taking place in the infield.

Ted tapped his foot impatiently as Hal changed lenses and continued to snap pictures. Finally, as the crowd began to descend the stairs and rush to the exit, he put the lens cap on his camera and stuffed it in his gadget bag.

"Okay, all done. Let's hit that great

Arby's stand for a sandwich on the way to the ag building."

"We're already fifteen minutes late, Hal. The girls'll get tired of waiting and leave if we don't hurry up. Then we'll never find them."

"Ah, come on. Just one quick sandwich. I'll even pay—and buy one for each of the girls, too."

The idea of Hal actually offering to buy the food was too much of a novelty for Ted to resist. "Well, okay, but we'd better make it snappy."

* * *

It was almost five when the boys hurried past the old-fashioned Coors beer wagon with its magnificent team of white-maned Belgians and into the main entrance to the agricultural barns. The sharp, not unpleasant smell of farm animals hit them as soon as they were through the wide door. The place was crowded with people wandering from stall to stall looking at the many breeds of horses on display. Pintos, Morgans, Arabians, Appaloosas, Welsh Ponies, even the little Miniatures were lined up in stalls along the side aisle. When they didn't find Tina and Trish waiting for them, they began to move down the aisle from one beautiful animal to the next.

When they finally came to the end of the aisle, Hal suggested they go down to where the cattle were penned. He especially wanted to get a look at the Simmentals which he'd heard so much about but had never seen.

"We can't Hal," Ted said, suddenly anxious about the girls. "We have to go back and look for Tina and Trish."

As they hurried back toward the main entrance, Hal panted, "I don't see them up ahead."

"Maybe they're in here watching the 4-H judging." Ted came to a stop at the door to a ringed arena. A group of kids about their age were solemnly checking out the calves in the inner circle and writing their marks on forms. The boys went inside and looked around. No Tina or Trish. "Darn, they must have got tired of waiting and left."

"They likely didn't even come in here," Hal laughed. "The smell was probably too much for Trish's sensitive nose."

Ted grinned back. "Yeah, you're right. Well, we can't do anything about it now so we might as well go back and check out the cattle. The girls will be waiting at the clock at six-thirty like Mom and Dad said."

But they weren't.

* * *

"It's almost seven o'clock," Mr. Harper reported, examining his watch for the tenth time in the last half hour. "What can be keeping the girls?"

"Maybe they got carried away looking at all exhibits in the Big Four Building and forgot the time," Ted suggested not too hopefully. It wasn't like his sister to be late for an appointment. Trish, maybe, but not Tina. He was worried and knew his mom and dad were, too.

Another fifteen minutes passed. Finally, Mrs. Harper got up from her bench under the clock and said, "Let's go on over to the grandstand. Perhaps the girls misunderstood and are waiting for us there."

The other three, anxious to do anything rather than sit around waiting, were quick to agree.

They hurried over to the plaza in front of the grandstand and began searching the faces of the many people milling about. There was no sign of the girls.

"They couldn't have gone into the grandstand," Mr. Harper reported. "I've got all our tickets.''

When the girls hadn't appeared by seven-thirty, Mr. Harper said bluntly, ''Okay, enough. I'm going to call the police.''

''Oh, George, will they take you seriously?'' his wife sighed. ''They'll likely think you're crazy reporting two missing girls at the Stampede.''

''They'd *better* take me seriously. Too much has happened already for me to believe that everything is just hunky-dory.'' And with that he strode into the enclosure under the grandstand to look for a phone.

Mrs. Harper and the boys found a bench under a tree and sat down to wait for him. No one spoke for a moment, each of them harbouring secret fears. Finally Mrs. Harper, trying for a distraction, reached in her purse and handed Hal an envelope.

''Here are the pictures you took in to be developed, Hal. Your uncle picked them up for you this afternoon.'' She got up and began to pace restlessly.

Hal tore open the envelope and pulled out the stack of pictures. Even his concern over Tina and Trish couldn't dull his eagerness to see how the five rolls of film he had shot since coming to Calgary had turned out.

He began to leaf through them quickly,

commenting on each one before handing it on to Ted. But Ted was not in the mood for a photography exhibit. He merely glanced at each picture, muttered, "That's nice," and passed it back.

Just as Hal was nearing the end of the pile Mr. Harper came hurrying across the compound. His wife rushed to meet him, calling out, "What did they say?"

"You were right about them not taking it too seriously," he reported angrily. "They said we should tell the park security to keep an eye out for the girls and that we should look for them ourselves. If they haven't shown up by ten o'clock, I'm to call them back."

"I was afraid of that," Mrs. Harper whispered, tears clouding her eyes. "Oh, George, if anything has happened to Tina or Trish, I'll never forgive myself."

"Now, now," Mr. Harper soothed. "We don't know that anything *has* happened. It could still be that the girls got distracted, as Hal suggested, and are trying to find us right this minute."

Hal and Ted nodded uncertainly and tried to smile. "Sure, Aunt Grace," Hal said. "We'll probably find them gazing at some dumb fashion show or listening to a rock group."

"I hope you're right. What do you suggest we do now, George?"

"I think the best thing is to split up. Ted, you and Hal check out the entertainment area and the Roundup Centre. Your mother and I will try the Big Four and the Saddledome. We'll meet right back here in an hour. If we haven't found them, I'm going to go to the police and *demand* they do something immediately."

"Right," Ted agreed, eager to be on his way. "Come on, Hal, we'll check the entertainment area first."

The boys began to thread their way through the crowds to the grassy area at the north end of the Park where a girl was standing on the stage singing an old Hank Williams number. There they split up and walked up and down the edge of the crowd trying to spot the girls in the audience. Ten minutes later when they met at the back of the crowd, it was obvious that neither of them had had any luck.

"Okay, let's head for the Roundup Centre," Ted ordered. "We'll split up again and cover all the aisles, then meet in the foyer."

Twenty minutes later Ted returned, dejected, to the foyer of the Roundup Centre where he found Hal sitting on a bench with a man in jeans and a leather jacket. To Ted's dismay, Hal was handing the man his new photos and talking a mile a minute.

"For Pete's sake, Hal," Ted yelled, "can't you think about anything but those stupid snapshots! Tina and Trish are missing and you're wasting your time— Oh, hi, Nick," he was very embarrassed. "I didn't recognize you at first."

"Hi, Ted. Hal told me about the girls. I'm sure they must be around here somewhere. It's a pretty big place and easy to get lost in."

Ted nodded mutely. He looked at Nick's drawn face and red eyes. "I guess there's no more news about Helen, eh?" he asked softly.

"No, nothing. Same with you?"

"Yep." He sat down on the bench beside Nick and cleared his throat. "Look, I know this sounds crazy, but I think that woman with the grocery cart is mixed up in this. At least, I know Tina thinks so." Ted stopped and shuffled his feet. "What I'm trying to say is that I have a feeling that Tina and Trish saw that woman here at the park and followed her. It's the kind of crazy thing Tina would do, and it sure explains why she and Trish didn't meet us when they were supposed to."

Nick stared at Ted a moment, then nodded his head. "I suppose it could be possible. But that doesn't help us much. The police don't know where Polly lives." He stood up and continued, "Look, I was just about to go over to the Palm Dairy stand for a cone. You guys want to join me? We can figure out what to do while we're eating."

"Great idea!" Hal cried and jumped up, scattering his pictures all over the floor.

Ted shook his head and bent down to help retrieve them. Hal was muttering under his breath about getting dirt on his best shots when Ted reached for a picture that had gone under the bench. As he picked it up he glanced at it, started to hand it to Hal, then grabbed it back and looked again. "I bet anything that's it."

"What's it?" Hal asked, reaching for the picture.

Ted looked up. Hal and Nick were staring down at him questioningly.

"This shot you took, Hal."

Hal looked down at the picture Ted was holding.

"Yeah, it's Amy. I snapped her when she wasn't looking, the day we went for dinner. What about it?"

“Look in the background. See the woman with the grocery cart? That’s Pop Can Polly.”

“So?” Hal asked. “We knew she was there that day. Tina saw her.”

“Yes, but she disappeared when we all turned to look at her.”

“Yeah, I remember. Really weird, wasn’t it?”

“Hal, don’t you get it? You caught her after Tina saw her. See, she’s turning into what looks like an alley.”

Hal took the photo and peered closely at it. “Yeah, I see what you mean. Polly probably lives somewhere down that alley.”

“Come on,” Nick ordered, heading for the exit. “My car’s in the lot behind the Park. We’ll check it out.”

CHAPTER 12

"There, up ahead," Ted cried. "That's the restaurant we went to."

Nick passed the restaurant and came to the alley. He braked and turned into the dark space between the two tall buildings. Then, easing the car along the almost black passage, he murmured, "Keep an eye out for anything unusual."

He hadn't gone more than ten metres when Hal yelled, "There! On the right. A door—and it's partly open."

Nick stopped the car and turned to the boys sitting beside him. "I'm going to go in and look around. It might be dangerous, so I want you guys to stay here. If I'm not back in five minutes go for help.''

Ted and Hal nodded solemnly, their eyes as big as saucers. Nick stepped out of the car and walked around to the door. He pushed it open with his foot and went inside.

* * *

''Did you hear that?'' Tina whispered.

''What? I didn't hear anything.'' Trish stifled a sob and raised her head to listen.

''There. Footsteps.'' Tina twisted on the bed trying for the hundredth time to loosen the rope that bound her to the bedpost. She had no idea how long they had been tied up. It seemed like a couple of days had passed, but she knew it was likely only a few hours. She was thirsty and had to go to the bathroom very badly. And she was terrified. What if Polly didn't tell anyone where they were? It could be days before anyone found them. They might even die before they were discovered.

But now there was hope. She had definitely heard movement in the next room. Was it Polly returning to free them? Or had she left the door open, and someone passing by saw it and decided to investigate?

Tina knew that whoever was out there could be dangerous, but she swallowed her fear and called out, "Help! We're in here."

Footsteps pounded across the outer room and the door flew open. A man stood in the doorway peering around the dim interior. It was Nick Gilbert.

"Nick! Here we are, over on the bed." Tina's voice shook with relief.

"What happened?" he cried as he rushed over and began cutting the ropes.

"It's Polly! She has Helen!" Tina rubbed her wrists where the rope had been chafing them.

"Where did they go?"

"We don't know. She just said she was taking Helen where no one could find her."

"But why?" Nick slashed the last of Trish's bonds and returned the knife to his pocket.

"We don't know that, either," Tina confessed. "But I'm pretty sure she was planning to take her out of town."

"Tina thinks Polly has some crazy idea about keeping Helen her prisoner—sort of like a trophy to look at and admire," said Trish.

"Sounds crazy, all right," Nick answered, "but I suppose it's as good an explanation as any. Come on, then. We'll call the police, then start looking ourselves. The boys are in the car just outside." He guided them through the dirty living room and out the door to the car.

When Ted saw Nick coming out with his sister in tow he jumped out of the car and ran to meet them.

"Tina, are you all right? Did that old woman do anything to you?"

"I'm fine, now, Ted—except for needing water and a bathroom," she added with a short laugh.

"And you, Trish? Are you okay?"

"I-I think so," Trish stammered. "But I've never been so scared in my entire life."

"Polly has Helen," Nick told the boys as Hal climbed out of the car. "We've got to get to a phone and call the police."

"There's a phone in the restaurant where we ate," Ted said. "I'll run down there. It's faster. Meet you guys out front." And with that he was off down the alley.

When the others arrived in the car, they could see Ted standing in a phone booth just inside the restaurant door, gesturing wildly. Nick jumped out and ran inside. He took the receiver from Ted's hand, spoke a few words, then hung up.

"We're to wait here for the police." Nick was back at the car relaying instructions. "Meantime, let's all go inside and you girls can tell us exactly what happened to you."

"Oh, boy! Let's go!" Tina groaned, grabbing the door handle. "I don't think I can hold on much longer."

After Trish and Tina returned from the restaurant ladies room, Trish began to tell their story. "Tina spotted Polly pushing her grocery cart when we were riding those little cars up above the grounds."

"Oh, my gosh!" Hal interrupted. "We've got to tell Aunt Grace and Uncle George that we found you. They'll be about out of their minds."

"It's okay, Hal," Nick smiled. "The police are taking care of it. There was a squad car already at the grounds. Mr. Harper called them when you didn't show up when you were supposed to." He turned back to Trish. "So then what happened?"

Between them the girls described everything that had happened after they had spotted Polly.

"Then she put Helen in a big canvas bag and carried her out of the room," Tina finished.

The expression on Nick's face turned to

horror.

At that moment, two squad cars roared up in front of the restaurant and four police officers, along with Mr. and Mrs. Harper, piled out.

"We've put an All Points Bulletin out for her," the man who had introduced himself as Sergeant Gariola announced when Nick and the kids came out to meet them. "We've got all the bus depots as well as the train station and airport covered."

"What about the roads out of town?" Nick asked.

"We have people on all the major routes, but she got a pretty good head start on us."

"Besides," Ted said, "it's not very likely that Polly owns a car or even knows how to drive one."

"Yeah," Hal agreed. "She probably carried Helen onto a bus. That's more her style."

"Well, we've done everything we can. Now, I'm afraid we'll just have to wait and see." Sergeant Gariola straightened up and motioned to the other officers. "Meantime, we'd like to take a look at the place where Polly was living. It might give us a clue or two." He turned to Mr. and Mrs. Harper. "Want to wait for us or can you get a lift with them?"

Nick said, "They can come with us. There's room if we all squeeze together."

The sergeant nodded and took off for the alley.

"We must get word to Charlotte and Helen's father immediately," Mrs. Harper said when the police had gone and they were piling into Nick's car. "Perhaps the best thing to do is go right home and call Mr. Gaynor from the house."

"Right," Nick agreed, whipping the car expertly into the traffic and heading for the suburb where the Harpers lived.

* * *

"I'll be right over," Helen's father barked and slammed down the phone.

Charlotte Gaynor turned to the others and relayed the message. She was barely able to speak. Ever since she had heard the news about Helen she had been in a state of shock.

"If only I had kept a closer eye on her, this never would have happened," she moaned, tearing at a limp handkerchief.

"That's just not true," Mrs. Harper said. "And you mustn't keep blaming yourself."

"But I feel so useless just sitting here. Isn't

there *something* we could be doing?"

"The police are doing everything possible," Nick assured her.

"Don't they have any idea where that awful woman might have taken Helen? Surely someone must know something about her."

"They may have found some clues when they searched her rooms," Nick answered. "We can only hope so. But all the police know about her at this point is that she came into town about a year ago and seemed to keep herself alive selling bottles and stuff. Social Service was told about her and offered help, but she apparently sent the worker scurrying off with threats of bodily harm."

This was not the most encouraging thing Nick could have said at the moment. Everyone thought immediately about what Polly might be doing to Helen.

Fifteen minutes later there was a knock on the door and Arthur Gaynor, not waiting for anyone to answer it, blew into the living room.

"Damn fool police!" he stormed, throwing himself down in a chair near the door. "They had the woman in custody and then let her go. I tell you, when this is all over some heads are going to roll."

Helen's aunt jumped to her feet and

started toward him. Then, obviously thinking better of it, she sank back into her chair and tried to look invisible.

"Now, tell me. What do the police know and what are they doing about finding my girl?"

Nick, with the help of the children, brought Mr. Gaynor up to date.

"Well, that woman must have said something that would give you a clue as to where she was taking Helen," he cried. "Think, damn it!"

"It won't do any good to shout and swear, Arthur," Charlotte scolded. "If it weren't for the children we would have no idea who had taken Helen. This way the police at least know who to look for."

Arthur Gaynor looked dumbfounded. Obviously he wasn't used to being criticized by his sister. He gazed uncomfortably at the Harpers, then turned to Nick.

"And how did you manage to get in the middle of this?" he snarled.

"I met the boys at the grounds when they were searching for Tina and Trish. When Ted saw the picture of Polly I drove them to the place where it had been taken."

"Yeah, if it hadn't been for Hal's photography and Ted's smarts, we might still be tied up to that bedpost!'' Tina couldn't contain her anger any longer. Helen's father seemed to think everyone but himself was some sort of fool.

Arthur Gaynor scowled at Tina. Slowly, the scowl turned into a reluctant smile. ''Right you are, little lady. I guess I needed someone to tell me that.'' He looked sheepishly around the room. Then, his eyes lit on Hal and, evidently anxious to make amends, he asked, ''May I see this famous picture, young man? I'd like to take a look at the woman who's caused me so much grief.''

''Sure,'' Hal replied, reaching in his pocket for the package of prints. ''But if you want to see what Polly looks like, I've got a great close-up of her I took at the parade.'' He began leafing through the pictures, then selected one and handed it to Mr. Gaynor. ''There she is. I got her with my telescopic lens.''

Arthur Gaynor took the print, glanced at it and turned white. ''Oh, no!'' he croaked, staring at the picture and shaking his head.

''Arthur, do you recognize the woman?''

''Yes, Charlotte, I recognize her,'' he sighed and slumped against the back of his chair, all the life seeming to drain out of him. ''It's Helen's mother.''

CHAPTER 13

The silence was almost tangible. Everyone stared at Mr. Gaynor. Then Charlotte jumped up from her chair and ran over to him. "Arthur, what's come over you?" she whispered, bending down and touching his shoulder. "Angela is dead. She died almost fifteen years ago."

"It's Angela," Arthur insisted. "I'd know her face anywhere. And she didn't die."

Charlotte took the picture from his hand and studied it carefully. "I admit that it certainly looks like her, but Arthur you have to face the fact that Angela DID DIE, no matter how much you would like to deny it."

"Damn it, woman, don't you understand?" Arthur Gaynor leapt to his feet and glared at his sister. "Don't any of you understand?" His gaze swept the room. "My wife didn't die; she left me. I couldn't face everyone knowing that I had driven her away so I made up a story about her being taken ill and being sent to the States where she died. No one questioned it. After all, Angela didn't have any family or friends to speak of. Besides, I didn't want Helen growing up thinking her mother had deserted her. It was best for her to think she was dead."

"I can't believe this!" Charlotte exclaimed. "All those years and you never told anyone; never tried to find her." She sank back in her chair and glared at him. "It's too much, just too much."

"But how come Helen didn't recognize her mother?" Ted asked, then answered his own question. "Oh, yeah, I guess she was too young to remember, eh?"

"She was only four when Angela left. Besides, her mother has changed a great deal since then. She used to be a beautiful woman, looked a lot like Helen does now, only taller. She's aged terribly, but I knew her immediately by her deep blue eyes." Arthur shook his head angrily. "If only I had some idea where she's taken Helen." Turning to Tina and Trish, he asked, "Are you sure she didn't say anything that might help us?"

The girls thought hard. "All she said was that she was taking Helen to a place where nobody would ever find her," Tina repeated. "Then she muttered something weird about the fall."

"What!" Arthur cried. "You didn't tell me that before. Now think! Exactly what words did she use?"

Tina and Trish concentrated for a moment. Then Tina spoke up. "She said, 'I'll keep her where nobody but me will see her.' Then she grinned this awful grin and said, 'And nobody will ever find her in the fall.' "

"Where's your phone?" he demanded. "I must get hold of the police immediately."

"There's one in the kitchen," Mrs. Harper answered, still in shock over his revelation. "But how can their knowing who Polly is help the police find her? They already know what she looks like."

"I am quite aware of that, madam. However, what the police don't know is where Angela—Polly, as you call her—took Helen."

"And you do?" Mr. Harper was skeptical.

"I do now," Arthur scowled, striding toward the kitchen door.

He came back a few minutes later, still

scowling.

"The sergeant in charge of the investigation isn't in," he reported. "I told the idiot who answered that I needed to get hold of him immediately, and he politely informed me he would get the message to this Gariola as soon as possible. Incompetent nincompoops!" he fumed. "Have to do their job for them." He turned to Nick. "Is that hotrod of yours in running order?"

"Of course," Nick answered.

"Then let's get going."

"Where?"

"TransCanada Highway. West. Old dirt road just outside Cochrane. I'll show you the way but hurry—we have no time to lose. I can't stand to think about what she's going to do to my girl!"

"If Polly really is Helen's mother," Tina asked in a doubtful voice, "then why would she want to harm her?"

"I think I know, but it's too complicated to go into right now." And with that he rushed out the door.

"Do you think he's gone round the bend?" Hal whispered to no one in particular.

"I don't think so," Charlotte answered. "It's quite possible that everything he said is true."

"At any rate, it sure can't hurt to go along with him," Nick remarked as he started to follow Arthur Gaynor out to the car.

"Hey, right on!" Ted and Hal chorused, jumping up and rushing after Nick.

Nick turned and held up his hand. "You kids can't come. It might be dangerous."

"Oh, come off it," Tina argued. "We've already been in about as much danger as we're likely to get into. You've just got to take us." She grabbed Trish by the arm and marched toward the door.

"Now, wait just one moment," Mr. Harper ordered. "You can't all go in Nick's car."

"But, Dad," Tina pleaded, "we *deserve* to be there when they rescue Helen. After all, if it weren't for us," she smiled triumphantly, "Helen might never have been found."

"The child's right," her mother agreed. "And I'm sure you want to go with them, too, Miss Gaynor. George, why don't you take her in Arthur's car? I'll stay here and try to get in touch with Sergeant Gariola."

So it was arranged that Nick would take Arthur and the two boys, while Mr. Harper would follow in Arthur's car with the girls and Helen's aunt.

* * *

"Now," Nick demanded as they sped down the highway, "it's time for some explanations. How can you be so sure you know where they are?"

Arthur Gaynor sighed and turned to look out the window. After a moment or two he spoke. "When Angela and I were first going out together we used to do a lot of exploring around the country. Both of us loved the outdoors and our courtship was conducted on picnics, horseback rides, boats. That sort of thing. One day when we were out hiking we stumbled across a little abandoned cabin way off the beaten track on a stream almost hidden from sight by a huge waterfall. The place was sturdily built, but had been badly neglected. Well, we made a vow that when we were married and settled down we'd find out who owned the place, see if we could buy it and make it our retreat from the world." He stopped to clear his throat and brush his hand across his eyes.

"We never did, though. Seems there was always so much to do. The ranch demanded more and more of my time and Angela was left pretty much on her own. Helen was born and for a while everything was fine again. Then I had a chance to buy the ranch next to ours and pretty soon I was back on the treadmill of work, sleep, eat and work again. Things weren't going too well for me. I thought I was going to lose both ranches. I suppose I wasn't too much fun to live with. We had no money for clothes or trips to the city or any of the things Angela loved. Anyway, after a while she began to act strangely: talking to herself, not keeping herself clean, eccentric sort of behaviour. We began to fight a lot. I demanded that she straighten herself out, but her behaviour got even more bizarre. Then one day I came home late and found her slumped in a chair staring into space and Helen sitting on the floor at her feet, dirty and crying for her dinner. She was centimetres away from a kitchen knife Angela must have dropped—or thrown—on the floor. I guess I went a little crazy—told Angela to clear out and never come back. I took Helen and stormed out of the house, thinking I'd take her into town for a meal while I cooled down.

"I realized I'd have to get help for my wife, and promised myself I'd talk to our family doctor the very next day. But when Helen and I got home a couple of hours later she was gone."

"But didn't you try to find her?" Ted asked.

"Oh, I tried—hired private detectives, the whole bit, but she just seemed to have disappeared from the face of the earth. Besides, even if I had known where she was I don't believe I could have persuaded her to come back. Too much bad had happened between us."

"And she just left Helen?" Nick asked. "That's hard to believe."

"I guess she knew she couldn't look after Helen properly. Maybe she even intended to come back for her one day. But you see, she really wasn't mentally sound even then. I don't suppose she really knew what she was doing." He sighed and slumped back against the seat. A moment later he was sitting bolt upright. "There, up ahead. Turn off on that road. We can go about four kilometres by car then we'll have to walk the rest of the way."

"What I don't understand," Ted frowned, "is how Polly—I mean Angela—could get Helen out here. You can bet she doesn't own a car."

"I suppose she just found one with the keys in the ignition and took it," Nick answered. "It's not that difficult, especially during Stampede when everyone is celebrating and not too careful."

They drove on for another few minutes,

passing no other cars on the almost impassable dirt trail. Then Arthur Gaynor signaled for Nick to slow down. "There's the creek. The waterfall should be around the next bend. If she did drive up here she may still be within hearing distance. We've got to take her by surprise."

Nick pulled the car over to the edge of the trail and stopped. The Harper car drew up a few metres behind and everyone piled out.

"Where to now?" Mr. Harper asked as Nick and the others came to meet them.

"We'll go the rest of the way by foot," Arthur answered. "Of course, they may not even be here." His face was drawn and he looked uncertain. "Perhaps I was wrong. She's probably forgotten completely about the cabin beside the falls."

"Well, there's only one way to find out," Nick said, starting up the hill. "Wait here and I'll take a look."

He disappeared around the bend. A minute passed, then another. Arthur started to follow him, but Mr. Harper held him back. "Wait, give him a little more time."

At that moment Nick reappeared up ahead and beckoned to them, his finger to his lips. As the group crept silently toward the bend in the road, he came to meet them.

"There's a car up ahead all right. It's parked behind a clump of trees. I would never have seen it if I hadn't been looking for it. There doesn't seem to be anyone around, but there are what looks like small tire tracks going away from it."

They followed Nick up the road and around the sharp bend. Nick pointed to the clump of trees and crept quietly toward it. They followed the tracks for another thirty metres or so until they came to the edge of a small creek. About fifteen metres up the creek, a tall waterfall cascaded. Everyone stopped and looked at Arthur.

"The cabin is behind those trees above the falls," he said pointing. "She must have taken Helen in some sort of carriage."

"Grocery cart," Trish and Tina chorused.

Arthur nodded and started toward the creek bed. "She has to be here all right," he agreed. "I only hope we're not too late."

CHAPTER 14

The cart tracks stopped at the bank of the creek, and the abandoned grocery cart lay half in the water. Arthur motioned for the group to follow him as he waded across the shallow water and headed up the steep incline toward a grove of trees at the top of the waterfall.

"How could Polly have carried Helen up here?" Mr. Harper panted as they stumbled and half-fell after Arthur.

"A desperate person will often have almost superhuman strength," Arthur answered. "And I expect Angela is very desperate."

At the top of the embankment, they entered the cool, dark shade of the elm trees growing beside the waterfall. Arthur pointed.

"The cabin is just up ahead. You'll see it when we come out of—"

"Don't anyone move."

The voice coming from behind was harsh and commanding.

The group came to an abrupt halt. Arthur Gaynor ignored the order and whirled around.

"Angela, for heaven's sake, what do you think you're doing?"

She waved a rifle menacingly and cried, "I told you not to move. Now turn around."

As he started toward her, Nick grabbed him by the arm and pulled him back.

"That's better," the woman said. "Now everyone put your hands over your heads and start walking."

They did as they were told and soon stepped out of the trees and into a clearing where an old log cabin stood.

"Open the door very slowly and go inside," the woman ordered when they reached the front of the cabin. They had no choice but to obey and found themselves in a large room with a dirt floor and a few rough pieces of furniture.

"All right you can turn around now." Angela stood in the doorway holding the rifle and grinning. "Thought you could creep up on old Polly, did you? I don't know who you nosy people are, but whoever you are, you'll wish you'd never tangled with me."

"Angela, don't you recognize me? It's Arthur."

She peered at the man standing before her with an agonized look on his face.

"Hmph. Don't know any Arthur." She let her gaze travel over the rest of the company. "You," she waved the gun at Tina and Trish. "Aren't you the two who came snoopin' around my house? Thought I had you all tied up."

The girls were too terrified to answer.

"Well, never mind. This time it won't be so easy to get away."

"Where have you got Helen?" Nick demanded.

Angela whirled around and stared at him, hatred distorting her features.

"You're the one in the picture, aren't you? The one who was going to take my Helen off —make her live like a hermit, just like *he* made me do. Well, it won't happen. Helen will never go through the hell I went through. No friends, no love." Her eyes glazed over and she stared into space. "Thought that man was a god. Turned out to be a devil."

"Angela, please," Arthur pleaded. "Don't do this. I never meant to cause you pain. I loved you."

"Shut up! All lies. No man ever tells the truth. All lies!"

"Angela, dear," Charlotte spoke soothingly, "please tell us where Helen is. You don't have to protect her from anyone."

Angela turned to her and frowned. "You're a stupid old maid, Charlotte Gaynor. What do you know?"

The captives were grouped in a semi-circle around the cabin. When Angela turned toward Charlotte, she turned her back on Tina and Trish.

"She recognized Helen's aunt," Tina whispered. "I bet she knows Mr. Gaynor, too."

Trish nodded. And started to whisper back.

"You two! Quiet!" The rifle swung around and pointed at Tina.

"What are you going to do with us?" Mr. Harper's cool voice broke in, taking Angela's attention away from his daughter.

"Never you mind. You'll find out soon enough." She waved the rifle again and said, "Everyone lie on the floor, face down."

Reluctantly they did as they were told.

"Now, don't anyone move. I've got this

rifle pointed right at you."

They all lay perfectly still. They couldn't see Angela from the angle at which they were lying. A minute passed, then another. They heard Angela move, then nothing. Finally, after another two minutes had passed, Ted couldn't stand it any longer. He raised his head and turned toward the door. It was closed and Angela was gone.

He jumped to his feet crying, "She's not here!" and ran to the door. He grasped the knob and it fell off in his hand. The others scrambled up and ran over to him. Nick pushed him gently aside and tried to put the knob back on, but it was useless. The door wouldn't budge.

"Locked from outside, I guess," Nick said, looking around for another escape route.

"There's a window here at the back," Arthur called, "but it's awfully small."

The others rushed over to where Arthur was pushing at a warped casing. After resisting for a moment or two the window shot up.

"It's so tiny," Ted moaned. "Nobody could get through there."

"I think I can," Trish said quietly. "I've got awfully small shoulders and hips and I'm practically double-jointed—ballet and gymnastics, you know."

"No! It's not safe!" Arthur Gaynor cried. "She may still be around, and if she sees you trying to escape she's very likely to shoot."

Totally ignoring the warning, Trish pulled a chair over to the window and eased herself out the small opening.

A moment later they heard her at the front door. The sound of metal against wood was followed by the door flying open. A triumphant Trish stood in the doorway.

"Gee! I didn't think you had it in you!" Ted grinned in admiration.

"There's lots you don't know about me, Ted Harper," she grinned back. "I'm more than just a pretty face!"

"We must find Angela before she harms Helen," Arthur cried.

"She won't hurt her own daughter surely?" Mr. Harper asked.

"I'm afraid she'll do anything to save Helen from what she thinks is a terrible life. If she thinks she can't hide her away, who knows what she may do? I've heard of people killing their children in cases like that. They're insane, of course, but, then so is Angela. We've got to find her before it's too late."

"Oh, no!" Charlotte Gaynor moaned.

"What are we to do?"

"Spread out and start searching," Nick answered. "She can't have gone far."

"Right," Mr. Harper answered. "But we'll have to move fast. It's starting to get dark. She'll be hard to spot before long. Miss Gaynor, you and the children stay here at the cabin. Lock yourselves in, in case she comes back this way. Meantime, I'll go north. Mr. Gaynor, you head west and Nick, you'd better go back the way we came—see if her car is gone."

The men left, and the kids and Helen's aunt huddled together in the entrance to the cabin.

After what seemed like an hour, but was less than a minute Ted said, "I don't know about you, but I can't just sit here and wait for something to happen. Come on, Hal, let's—"

"Shh!" Tina put her finger to her lips. "I think I heard something."

Silence.

"There. It's coming from behind the cabin. Quick! Get inside and close the door."

They only just made it. Peering through a crack in the door they saw Angela coming around the side of cabin. She had the canvas bag slung over her left shoulder and the rifle under her right arm.

"What'll we do?" Tina whispered frantically.

"Follow her, of course," Ted answered. "Helen's in that canvas bag—probably still alive or she wouldn't be carrying her so carefully."

When Angela entered the woods, Ted and Hal crept out of the cabin and, keeping a good distance between them, began to follow her.

Angela plodded on without turning back. In a very short time she had reached the top of the waterfall.

The boys, close behind, peered cautiously around a large fir to see which way she had gone. They thought they had lost her at first, then to their horror they saw that she had waded into the creek and was standing at the edge of the falls where the turbulent water plunged over the rocky embankment.

Looking neither right nor left, she calmly tossed the rifle onto the bank and slung the canvas bag off her shoulder.

"Ted, she's going to throw Helen over the falls!" Hal whispered. "What'll we do?"

Ted's mind raced. If he could just get to the rifle before Angela saw him there was a chance he might be able to scare her into bringing Helen back to shore. On the other hand, if she did see him, she would surely act quickly, and once Helen was sent over the falls her chances of coming out of it alive were practically nil. But he had to take that chance. There was no other way.

Luckily, Angela seemed to be having trouble opening the canvas bag, which gave him some precious time.

"Hal, you'll have to go back up and cross the creek to the other side. Then when you get back down here, do something to get her attention so I can grab the rifle."

Hal headed up the creek and waded to the far side. Ted heard his yell a moment later, and then saw Angela turn, startled, toward the sound. In an instant, Ted was rushing toward the rifle. As his hand reached out to grab it, his foot hit a loose stone and he lost his balance. Before he knew what was happening he was rolling down the steep embankment.

He came to a halt halfway down. His knee was bleeding and he felt like his wrist might be sprained. He stood up and started back up the bank. And there ahead of him stood Angela, her rifle aimed at his chest.

CHAPTER 15

Ted looked up at her in terror. She began to move toward him. Out of the corner of his eye he could see the canvas bag resting precariously against a rock at the top of the falls. The slightest movement would send it careening over.

"Please, Mrs. Gaynor, don't shoot me. I only wanted to help Helen," he pleaded.

"Helen doesn't need your help, young man. I'm taking care of my baby now. Helen is going to be safe forever. She will never be hurt like I was."

She moved closer. "Too bad you had to interfere. I don't particularly want to hurt you and that other bunch up in the cabin, but

I guess I have no choice." She lifted the rifle and started to take aim.

Then everything seemed to happen at once. He saw the canvas bag start to move. In a second it would be freed from the rock that was holding it back and tumbling over the falls. Then from behind Angela, Hal came into view, and at the same time Nick's head appeared over the top of the embankment on the right.

Ted knew he had to keep her talking to give Nick time to get to her.

"But why do you think Helen needs to be safe?" he asked desperately.

"Because the same thing was happening to her that happened to me. And I won't permit it." Angela moved closer and lowered the rifle. Ted could see from her eyes that she was quite mad.

"She was parading around. I had to stop that. I did the same when I was her age, and it brought me nothing but grief and pain. Then I read in the paper she's already got herself engaged. A rancher just like her father!" She laughed mirthlessly. "Oh, yes, the sins of the mother were being visited upon the daughter. She would have ended up exactly as I had. But I saved her from that. And nobody is going to stop me."

She raised the rifle again but she had waited too long. Nick was down the embankment. As she pulled the trigger, he lunged at her arm and the bullet fired harmlessly into the air. Hal dove for the canvas bag and stopped it slipping away from its moorings just as Angela dropped the rifle, twisted out of Nick's grasp, and ran back up the embankment. Nick and Ted scrambled up after her but she was too quick for them. She reached for the canvas bag, swatted Hal away with her free hand, and began to pull the bag, with Helen still inside, into the middle of the stream. Nick and Ted were close behind her when the bag broke loose.

"Too late!" she cried and started to send the bag toward the edge of falls.

Instantly Nick was on her. He pushed her roughly aside and grabbed the bag just as it was about to tumble over the falls. Angela lunged desperately toward him, but she stumbled on some slippery stones at the edge of the creek and before anyone could help her she had plunged over the edge of the falls.

When they finally reached her she was lying in a twisted heap in the shallow creek at the bottom.

Nick pulled her from the water, bent over

her and put his finger on her neck. "She's dead," he said quietly.

"What's going on?" a voice called, and Arthur Gaynor, along with Mr. Harper, stumbled out of the woods. "We thought we heard a shot."

Arthur ran over to where his wife lay, and gasped. "Is she . . . ?"

"I'm afraid so," Ted whispered.

"Oh, Angela!" He fell on his knees beside her.

Meantime Nick was tearing at the clasps of the canvas bag. "Please let Helen be all right!" he groaned. The flap broke free and he pulled the still unconscious girl out and placed her gently on the ground, where she lay white and unmoving.

Mr. Gaynor rushed up behind him. "Is she all right?" Without waiting for an answer, he pushed Nick away and began to call to her. "Helen! Helen! Please wake up." He slapped her gently on the cheek and continued to try to rouse her. The girls and Charlotte, having heard the rifle shot, arrived on the scene.

Charlotte took the situation in with one quick glance and rushed to Helen's side. "Out of the way, Arthur. Let me look at her." She bent over Helen, felt her pulse, lifted her eyelids and listened to her heart. "She's alive, but her heartbeat is weak. I suspect it's the combination of the knock-out drops Angela gave her and the lack of air in that bag. And shock. We must get her to a hospital right away."

Without another word, Nick picked Helen up in his arms. "Mr. Harper, run and bring the car as close as you can, please." And he walked down the incline and across the creek, with Helen's father and aunt close behind.

"What about Angela?" Ted asked. "We can't just leave her here like this."

"We'll send someone back for her when we get to town," Charlotte answered. "Right now, Helen is the only thing that matters."

Nick lay Helen gently in the back seat and got in beside Mr. Harper. Charlotte climbed in the back where she could keep an eye on Helen. They were about to set off when a car came roaring around the bend in the road, sirens screaming.

"Thank goodness! It's the police," Charlotte cried.

The police car roared up and Sergeant Gariola and another officer jumped out. Nick quickly explained what had happened.

"We've got to get help for Helen immediately," he finished. "Can you give us an escort back to town?''

"You bet! Let's get moving.'' Sergeant Gariola jumped back into the squad car and roared off. Mr. Harper gunned the motor and took off behind him.

Helen's father turned to the kids. ''Jump in,'' he said. ''I don't know if I can drive this hotrod of Nick's but I'm sure going to try.''

* * *

Mrs. Harper was on the front porch waiting when Mr. Harper and the kids drove up to the house an hour later.

''What happened?'' she cried running out to meet them. ''Did the police find you? I gave them the best directions I could.''

They climbed wearily out of the car and Mr. Harper put his arms around her.

''It's all over, dear. Helen is safe. She's at the Foothills Hospital, but she should able to leave tomorrow. Her father and aunt are staying there with her, as, of course, is Nick.''

He started to walk toward the house still embracing his wife. ''We'll tell you all about it when we get inside. I don't know about the kids, but I could sure use a cup of hot chocolate.''

CHAPTER 16

It was Monday afternoon, and Trish and Hal would soon be on a plane to Toronto. A whole crowd had come to the airport: Tina and Ted, Mr. and Mrs. Harper, Amy and Rhonda, Arthur and Charlotte Gaynor, Nick and Helen.

"Gee, I wish we were coming instead of going," Trish sighed. "I can't believe we've been here nearly two weeks."

"Yeah," Hal agreed. "It was the best holiday I've ever had."

"And the scariest," Trish added.

"Okay, everybody, get in a group," Hal ordered, focusing his camera. "I've got to get a parting shot."

"Oh, groan!" Tina said. "It's bad enough you have to take gross pictures of us. Now you're making bad puns."

"Sure, knock it," Hal answered. "But if it hadn't been for my photography . . ."

"You're right, Hal," Helen smiled. "I probably wouldn't be around."

Nick shuddered and put his arm around Helen. "Amen to that," he murmured.

"The hardest thing is accepting the fact that my own mother would try to kill me," Helen said, when Hal had finished taking several pictures. "I'll never understand that."

"Helen, dear, your mother was mentally ill," her father answered. "She thought she was doing what was best for you. Remember all those newspaper articles about you the police found in her rooms? It must have unbalanced her even further to realize that the Stampede Queen was her own daughter, the one she had abandoned years ago."

Helen nodded and moved closer to Nick. "It's funny but I could honestly feel something between us." She turned to Tina and Trish. "Remember at her place when I had the knife and I couldn't use it? It was as though I knew she was more than just some crazy woman."

No one spoke for a moment; each of them thinking about the events of the past week. Then Hal broke the silence.

"So when are you guys getting married?" he asked.

"Not till next spring," Helen answered. "And you're all coming to the wedding."

"That's right," Nick chimed in. "And Hal's going to be the official photographer."

Hal beamed like he'd just been handed an Olympic gold.

"The wedding will be at the ranch," Arthur Gaynor said, "and we want you kids to come down and stay with us a while after it's over. It's going to be lonesome with Helen gone even if she is just a short distance away." He smiled fondly at his daughter. "It's been a terrible experience for all of us, especially you, my dear, but when all's said and done, it has certainly turned out for the best. Oh, I don't mean Angela's death, of course," he hastened to add. "That was tragic. But the experience brought home to me just what I was doing to Helen. I'll never be able to forgive myself for the pain I caused Angela, but at least I was stopped from repeating it."

"Yeah," Hal added, "it *did* all turn out okay. Nick won the saddle bronc event;

Helen got to be Stampede Queen again; and we *finally* got to see the grandstand show!"

"It's almost time for the plane to leave," Mr. Harper warned them. "We'd better get you kids boarded before it takes off."

Trish kissed everyone while Hal started to shake hands. But Amy wasn't having any of that. She bent down and gave Hal a big kiss on both cheeks. Helen and Rhonda immediately followed suit. Hal was so shook up he dropped his camera then bumped heads with Amy who bent over to pick it up for him. By the time they got everything sorted out, Ted and the girls were laughing so hard they could barely make it to the barrier.

As they settled down in their seats, Trish sighed.

"That's the most exciting time I've ever had, Hal. Home is going to seem so dull after this. I guess we used up a whole lifetime of thrills in just ten days."

"Not quite," Hal said, pulling out the snack bag Mrs. Harper had prepared for them. "We've still got these!"

And to Trish's dismay, he extracted a handful of chocolate chip cookies and began munching them before the plane even left the ground.

MARY BLAKESLEE

Mary Blakeslee's warmth, humour and caring spirit are projected in her writing for young people. Her fast-paced style makes for compelling reading and is the result of several years of honing her writing skills.

Since the early 1980s, Mary has devoted herself to writing full-time. Her unique talent has resulted in several well-received books, including *Wheelchair Gourmet, It's Tough to be a Kid, Halfbacks Don't Wear Pearls, Edythe with a Y, Carnival* and *Will to Win.*

Mary is a graduate in Social Work from the University of British Columbia. She has been a consultant with the Department of Education in Manitoba. She now lives in Calgary with her husband, Clem. When she's not writing, her hobbies include photography and gourmet cooking.